RYKO

Second edition. For Gav.

Book design by: www.AnnetteWoodGraphics.com

ISBN 978-0-578-86772-4

www.WhiskerLife.com

Whisker Life™

LOVE MORE.
HISS LESS.

FOR MY MOM AND DAD.

INTRODUCTION

YOU KNOW, it's not easy writing your own story. Especially when your heart tells you that your real story is only about to begin.

Part of me feels much of this should always be kept locked up in my memories, never to be shared with a soul. But there's another part of me that is pushing me to get my story out into the world. *You can guess which side won.*

I feel it's important for me to share everything that has happened to me up to the point of writing and finishing this book. If nothing else, I hope to inspire others to go out on their great journey because you just never know what you'll find or who you will meet.

Sometimes it can take one single event, which seems meaningless at the time, or meeting just one cat to completely alter the direction of your life forever. Sometimes that can happen multiple times, in a very short period of time, as I learned the hard way.

So to begin, please allow me to introduce myself. My name is Ryko. I'm the Founder of a new adventure called, Whisker Life™.

At the time of this writing, Whisker Life is in the process of all coming together. I'm working very hard to hopefully open our doors soon.

I have very big dreams, plans, and goals for Whisker Life. In fact, I've been preparing for it all my life, well, sort of. The reality is that life has been preparing me for it. I just didn't see or understand that until only recently. You'll see what I mean shortly.

What you are about to read is a true story. I can vouch for everything that happened because it happened to me.

This is the story of my life. So far.

ENTRY 1

LIFE IS INTERESTING, isn't it? Sometimes when everything around you is perfect, it can all come crashing down. Yet, there are other times when everything is upside down, and it can all flip around and be made perfect again in a matter of seconds.

Let's just be honest. Maybe *interesting* isn't the best word to use. Let's just call it what it is… IT'S WEIRD.

Now I don't know about you, but I've certainly been through my fair share of flips, as well as flops. And each one has taught me a valuable lesson that I carry with me to help me on my journey. And of course, to keep the journey interesting, the lessons we learn aren't always apparent right away. Sometimes it can take days, weeks, months, or years to figure out why something happened.

Yet there are moments when a lot of time has gone by and you still can't figure it out. Those lessons drive me crazy. Patience, Ryko. Patience.

Looking back at my journey that has led me to this very moment, some of the right-side-up and upside-down parts make sense now. But I'll be totally real with you. At times, and boy there were a lot of those times, I had no idea what I was doing, let alone which direction I was going. I just always felt deep down I was going somewhere amazing.

I just didn't know how to get there, or even if this "somewhere" really existed.

Let me ask you something... Have you ever had the feeling that there was something more for you in life? And the more that you searched for it, the more it eluded you?

It's like this nagging feeling that something just doesn't feel right, or that something within you isn't complete. I don't know about you, but I spent a lot of time trying to find the root cause of that feeling that was deep inside of me.

It drove me nuts sometimes. As soon as I thought I was starting to figure it out, something would happen or the feeling would go away completely for awhile, only to return again at the craziest of times.

But I finally did it. I finally figured it out. And it took far longer than I ever thought it would. I traveled down the toughest paths you could ever imagine. Coming face to face with the root cause of that feeling was the most terrifying thing I've ever done, and probably will ever do.

But the journey is worth it. Oh boy, is it worth it. Please believe me on this one. No matter where your journey takes you, it's the path you were meant to travel down. Yes, you may fight it at times. Sometimes it will feel and seem to be nearly impossible. And there will be times where everything flows smoothly and everything in between comes together.

But no matter what happens, no matter how good or bad things get, stay the path. Even when you have no idea where you're going or why you're still looking. Just keep moving forward.

ENTRY 2

I JUST DIDN'T KNOW how to get there, or even if this "somewhere" really existed.

But it does exist. Low and behold, the story is actually true. Everyone thought it wasn't real, but it is. It truly is. I've seen it with my very eyes. I've breathed the air. I've walked the grounds and trails. I've seen the glistening trees. I've sipped from the sparkling lake.

Yes, it does exist, despite what everyone else has told you. There truly is a place, just as the book describes. And it is even more magical, more magnificent, and more beautiful than you could ever imagine.

In fact, I'm writing these very words sitting on the exact rock by the majestic oak tree on the hill, just as York (you'll learn more about him later) described in perfect detail. From here, I have a perfect view of the valley he described. The rolling meadows, the sparkling lake, the mountains with the glistening trees in the distance, the sweet, crisp air. IT IS REAL. All of it.

Now I'm sure you have questions and lots of them. And I don't expect you to believe me right now. But I can assure you, what I'm telling you is true.

But before we go too far down that path, I invite you to walk with me on my path. Because how I ended up here is nothing short of a miracle. And what I'm doing here... Well, I'll explain that soon enough.

But first, let me take you back several years ago... to a time when life was much more simple. So simple, in fact, it was purrfect.

ENTRY 3

MY FATHER, KENNO, is a fearless cat who lived in a small town outside of Richmond, Virginia. There wasn't a cat around who would dare cross his path, but he also had a lesser known gentle side that was full of love. Honestly, he would never hurt a soul.

He would spend most of his days playing in his backyard, and then at night, he would curl up in a ball on his favorite blanket.

One day, my father decided it was time to go on his journey. He traveled far and ended up in New Hampshire. In fact, he liked it there so much, he decided that Franklin, New Hampshire would be his new home.

He absolutely loved it on Terrace Road. He had a small, one-story brick house with two large picture windows in the front that he loved looking out of. His house was on top of a small hill and he loved spending his days running up and down that hill.

Not too far from his home was a small downtown with little shops that lined both sides of the street. There were old railroad tracks that went through town along with an old train station.

It was such a great place to live. Well, during the spring, summer, and fall, that is. The winters were certainly pretty tough and very cold. The snow and cold seemed to last too long, and the summers were always too short. But when the weather was good, it was perfect.

A few years went by, and another cat moved into the blue house next door Kenno. Her name was Robin, and she was the most beautiful cat in town. She was the kindest, sweetest, and most loving cat you could ever meet.

Robin and Kenno, or as I call them, Mom and Dad, quickly fell in love. After they got married, my Mom moved into the brick house with my Dad, and it wasn't too long after that that I was born.

Being an only cat sure did have its benefits. While most of my friends had many brothers and sisters, it was just me and my parents. We spent all of our time together. From morning to night, we embarked on adventures, played, and just enjoyed life without a care in the world.

When I was a kitten, my parents used to drive me a little crazy because of all the cuddles, hugs, and kisses they gave each other. Even when we were out in public and they kissed, I would always say, "Ewww mom and dad, STOP!"

But as I got a little older, I started to understand and see what they had. It was truly one of the rarest loves any cat could ever find. You could feel the love whenever you were around them. And as crazy as it sounds, other cats could, too.

Whenever we all walked in a store or restaurant with other cats, my parents would walk in and all eyes would be on them for a moment when they entered. I know the other cats could sense that my mom and dad had something truly special, unique, and rare. And me being grossed out turned into me being proud for having such amazing parents that had something so special.

For as long as I can remember while growing up, my parents always told me that I was a very special cat; that I was destined for great things that would help others around the world. In fact, I heard it so many times that I not only started to believe it, but I started to wonder what those great things could be.

Not long after I started to wonder, a strange feeling in my belly that something wasn't quite right would come and go. It was like I was missing something... or someone... or some... I didn't know exactly.

Every night before bed, pretty much since the day I was born, my mother would read me stories from a large collection of books that were in the barn. There were books covering every subject you can think of.

From books about space to lizards. Egypt to sharks. Mice to gardening. My parents and I loved to read, especially during those New Hampshire winters.

Out of the hundreds of books we read, there was always one that I asked for each and every night since the first time my mom read it to me.

And that book was called, "Whisker Hollows."

That book spoke to me in a way that lit up all of my senses. It made me so excited about life and possibilities. I always had trouble going to sleep after, but I didn't mind. I felt that the book was written for me because it made me feel like I was there and that anything I set my mind to was possible.

ENTRY 4

THE WHISKER HOLLOWS BOOK was a story about a cat named York, a name also shared by the author. He was a cat whose life started out pretty hard. Abandoned as a kitten, he had to find his own way and make his own way. He ended up living on the streets in a large city for several years.

Later on, he bounced around from one shelter to the next, never really having a place to call home. Throughout his time in the shelters he made some friends, but it seemed like every time he did, he shortly had to move to a new shelter and start all over again.

One day, York was being transported to yet another shelter, and there was a bad storm. The town began to flood, and every cat swam for their lives. York ended up swimming over to a tree, climbed up, and waited for the flood to be over. Then once it was safe to go back down, York decided it was time to go on his journey.

For the next few years, York got to travel the country. Sometimes by train, but mostly by paw. He learned how to catnap and became interested in how our minds and the world around us works. He had no desire to return to the busy city, so he set out to find a quiet place to relax and live a much more peaceful life.

One day, while walking down a long-forgotten path, he found himself in a forest which was unlike anything he had ever seen. As he continued to walk, the air around him began to change. As he breathed in the sweet, crisp air, a feeling of absolute happiness began to take over him

Little did he know that he stumbled upon a long-forgotten place that was truly magical. It was a place where anything and everything was possible. It was where our dreams went and turned into reality. A place where just breathing in the sweet, crisp air made your entire being swell with happiness.

There was a wide-open field, with rolling hills as far as the eye could see. There were tall mountains that had trees with leaves that glistened in the sunlight. There was a lake that sparkled like diamonds. And there was a forest filled with walking trails and ruins of an ancient civilization that once called this very special and unique place home.

Now this place was not only where dreams went to become reality, but it was also one of the sources of happiness. In fact, so much happiness radiated from this place that it could be felt from the other side of the world, but only if you knew how to connect to it.

As the story goes, the name of this special place didn't come from York. It had already been named long, long ago. He spent several days exploring forests, ruins, and valleys. Then one day, while looking for a place to catnap, York attempted to climb on a rock and slipped on some moss. Part of the moss fell off of the rock, uncovering a "W" and an ' H."

As York removed the moss, the word "WHISKER" appeared, followed by "HOLLOWS" under it. Apparently, it looked like it had been carved into the rock a very, very long time ago.

In the book, *Whisker Hollows*, York said that there were dozens of secrets hidden all across the land that taught sacred knowledge, also known as wisdom. The secrets and wisdom they contained had great power. Power to turn dreams into reality. Power to accomplish your goals quickly. Power to catnap deeper than ever before. Power to truly let go of one's past and start anew.

In the book, York didn't talk too much about the knowledge found in Whisker Hollows, but he did say that over the course of many years and several lifetimes, he gained more than 49 bits of wisdom. Wisdom that changed everything. In fact, he said that learning and truly understanding just one of the insights was more than enough to live a complete life.

I've always wondered what secrets Whisker Hollows held and what knowledge York had gained. More importantly, I wondered and asked my parents constantly why York didn't share them in the book.

There were a lot of things that I connected with in the *Whisker Hollows* book. But there was one part that truly stuck with me. York warned that Whisker Hollows wasn't for everyone. It was a place only for those who wanted to find their true purpose and their source of happiness with all of their heart. But for those who did find their way to Whisker Hollows, an unimaginable life awaited them.

As you can imagine, as a kitten and young adult, I was mesmerized by *Whisker Hollows*. I asked my parents a thousand times if Whisker Hollows was real and if we could go find it. They always told me that the book was a story. One to inspire people to find their own Whisker Hollows within themselves.

And as much as I wanted to believe their explanation, I always wondered… What if some of the story was real? What if all of it was real?

As I got older I learned that when the *Whisker Hollows* book was first published many years ago, it was a pretty big deal. There were stories of cats who embarked on adventures to search for Whisker Hollows. Many went alone while others had dozens of cats with them and went on great expeditions into the forest.

The book started to become such a distraction that the publisher actually recalled the book. The books were removed from all the shelves and the publisher even paid people ten times the cover price to mail the book back to them.

They say that there are only a handful of *Whisker Hollows* books out there today. But sadly, it's a long-forgotten story. If you go up to someone today and ask them what they think about Whisker Hollows, no one knows what you are talking about. It's sad, really.

To be honest, I've asked a lot of other cats over the years about *Whisker Hollows*. Strangely, I've yet to find anyone who has read the book, and only a few older cats who remember hearing about cats searching for a lost land or some sort of treasure, but nothing more.

And finally, on the last page of the book, there was a poem York wrote that I memorized and have repeated countless times in my head. He said he wrote this after an experience he had in the forest that surrounds Whisker Hollows. Here's what the poem says:

Title: Whisker Hollows Awakens
By: York

Scattered chaos; life unfulfilled,
Dreams broken, an urge to rebuild.
Darkest night; unbearable days,
Gives birth to light, casts self ablaze.

Awakened mind; weathered soul,
A fire burns, without coal.
Eyes wide open; ego closed shut,
Random events, strings uncut.

Energy waves; vibration flows,
Endless searching, fading woes.
Unknown paths; newfound roads,
Life rearranges, inner-self implodes.

R Y K O

Greater knowing; quantum seeing,
Loss of self, life takes meaning.
A deep breath; nature's true song,
A new life begins, we knew all along.

Rustling stars; prevailing breeze,
Yearning for more, missing keys.
Kindred spirit; ineffable desire,
Only love can ignite the fire.

Sacred stone; soft rolling hills,
Glistening leaves, water fulfills.
Sacred knowledge; ancient clues,
Follow your heart, it's time to choose.

ENTRY 5

I REMEMBER EVERYTHING. It's as if I relived the same exact day a thousand times. Because in many ways, I have. I remember specifically one morning waking up: The sun was out, the birds were chirping, and there was a soft, cool breeze flowing through the trees.

The smell of my mother's pancakes filled the house. I could hear my father whistling and chopping wood out back by the shed. I got out of bed, stretched, walked out into the kitchen, and sat down at the table.

Within seconds, my mother had put a large stack of pancakes in front of me. Oh how I loved those pancakes.

In New Hampshire we had access to endless apples, my mother's secret ingredient. I could put down a stack of pancakes faster than three shakes of a tail.

But that morning was different. As I ate my pancakes, I looked out the window. I don't know if it was just the right angle of the sun peeking through the trees, or if it was some higher calling, but what

I saw made me drop my fork onto the table.

Through the trees was a single ray of light that went across the yard, through our window, and onto a book. And I knew exactly what book it was because I had left it there the night before. It was *Whisker Hollows*. As I looked at the tiny ray of sunlight, as it cast itself upon the book, I nearly let out a giant meow.

Through the branches of the trees, or the leaves, or the window, or who knows what, that little ray of light became two smaller rays of light on the book. And as crazy as it sounds, the light created two perfect letters under the *Whisker Hollows* title.

The letters were G and O.

And the second I read "GO," the light vanished.

Later that morning, as I walked through the forest to one of my favorite places to catnap, I could not stop thinking about what I saw. What were the odds of something like that actually happening? For me to leave the book there. To have it angled slightly facing the breakfast table. For the sun to be in that exact spot. For the branches to be perfectly aligned. For the window to be opened only half-way that morning. The odds were simply a trillion to one. At least.

As I walked, I allowed my mind to wonder on the other side. What if it was a sign? What if something or someone was telling me to go? To go to Whisker Hollows? Am I crazy? It doesn't even exist. Or does it? How is this even happening? Maybe my mind was just playing tricks on me? Maybe it was just a simple sunbeam and I imagined the light creating the letters?

Needless to say, my catnapping session that morning went nowhere. I could not quiet my mind, no matter how hard I tried and no matter which technique I used. I decided to walk back home.

By the time I got back, my father had just finished lunch and asked me if I wanted to bat the ball around with him, like we always did in the afternoon. (By "bat the ball around," I, of course, mean playing our favorite game: cat ball.) I agreed and we walked over to the side of the house.

My father was more of a quiet cat. But when he spoke, everyone listened. He just had a way with words that made you feel cared for and appreciated. He also had quite a knack for picking up on things when they weren't quite right with someone. Sometimes it drove my mom and I crazy, because it was like he knew something was wrong with us even before we knew it ourselves.

As we walked to the side of the house, my father stopped and looked at me with his big green eyes. "I know something is puzzling you, son," he said. Like countless times in the past, I knew there was no hiding or escaping it. I had no choice but to share what had happened to me that morning and all the crazy thoughts and questions I had running through my mind.

As I told the story, I remember thinking how surprised I was by my father's facial expressions. Part of me felt like he was going to laugh, but his expression was the one he made when I did something that made him proud of me.

When I finished telling him about the sunbeam on the book, he started walking over to the ball and batted it over to me. I batted it back. We continued this for a few minutes and he stopped the ball.

"I think you are ready, son," my father said.

"I'm ready for what?" I asked.

My father stood up and said, "You're ready for the journey, son. Back when I was your age, I had a tickle to see what was out there in the world. I wanted to explore past my yard. Past my neighborhood. Out into the unknown. I wanted to see how others were living and just be free."

I walked over to my father. "So you are saying that I'm ready to go out and see the world and go out on my journey?" I asked.

"Yes, you are," my father said with a huge smile and gave me the biggest hug. "But it is not for me to decide. You must know in your mind and heart if it is time." I hugged my father. I could feel that it was time to go on my journey.

"You're right, father, I feel it in my heart. It is time," I said.

Later that evening, my mother was cooking dinner and I walked by the kitchen on my way to the bathroom to clean myself up.

"Ryko, I hear you're going to be going on a trip? You better fill up tonight. I'm making your favorite," my mother said with a big smile. I guess word traveled fast.

Thinking about it, I knew the day was coming soon. After all, that's how life works for all cats. We're kittens, then we get a little older, and we go on our journeys. It's basically the step right before adulthood that we all must go on to find our calling in life. Or at least, that's the goal.

Now don't get me wrong, going out on our own is a very good thing. It's how we cats find ourselves, learn what we want to do for jobs as adults, and many cats find their mates when they are on their journeys. So believe me, I had a lot of things to be very excited about. After all, the female cat choices were pretty limited in my neighborhood. When I mean limited, I mean zero. There were no female cats my age within a few miles from me.

During dinner that evening, my parents and I talked about my journey and they told me stories about their own journeys that I had never heard before. It was a night full of laughs, cries, and plenty of meows.

We all knew that I had to leave the next day because, well, that's how it works. One of the rules we cats all follow is that the day a cat is ready for his journey, he or she packs their bags and leaves the next morning. It's always been that way, and it will always be that way. As the saying goes, "It's not who we are the day we leave for our journey, it's who we become because of the journey."

Later that night, my parents pulled out a couple of their journals they had written in on their own journeys, shared more stories, photos, drawings, and also gave me my own journal to take on my journey.

I filled up the first three or four pages with notes and advice that my parents shared. I'll share a few with you now...

Follow my heart instead of the road.

The roads are the paths of many. Very well-traveled. It's the safest route. Follow those roads and you end up where everyone else is. If you follow your heart, become a trailblazer, and claw your own path in the wild, well, that's where the real journey begins.

Never trust a white cat in an alley in the middle of the city.

This one was from my father. Apparently, he met a white cat while walking around in a city called Denver. He took a wrong turn and ended up in an alley. After talking to a white cat he met in the alley, the cat gave a nod, and before my father knew it, five other cats jumped on him and tried to steal his backpack. They beat him up pretty bad, but in the end, my father was the only one to walk out of that alley. And he still had his backpack.

Keep an open mind and a wide-open heart.

My mother told me this, followed by the story of how she had pretty much given up trying to find true love on her journey. She came back home, packed up, and moved to New Hampshire to just live a peaceful life and eat apples.

Although she had given up searching in her mind, she kept her heart wide open for the possibility. Soon after my father came into the picture, as I've been told a million times, it was love at first meow. Yes, my parents both knew literally the second their eyes met that they were destined to be together.

The moral of this lesson is that even if your mind wants to give up, you have to make sure you never close your heart. A closed heart closes all possibilities. After all, we know our minds are like a runaway train, most of the time anyway. We don't have full control of that. But, we do have control of keeping our hearts open.

ENTRY 6

THAT NIGHT, I BARELY SLEPT. I was nervous, excited, scared, anxious, and honestly, ready for my journey to begin.

As the faintest bit of light began to fill the eastern horizon, I got out of bed and went over to my window. I stood and watched the sky become lighter and lighter as the sun began its own journey. Crickets chirped their melodies to one another as if they were performing a beautiful symphony.

After a short while, one bird started chirping, and then another. I never realized how peaceful it was in the morning right at sunrise. The morning dew drops began to glisten in the sunlight, as the fog began to lift from the ground.

Lost in my own thoughts, I didn't hear my parents come into my room. I don't know how long they were standing there, watching me, but I was startled when I heard a little sniffle. I jumped, turned around, and my mother and father were standing there, arm in arm, with giant smiles on their faces.

My mom ran over to me and gave me a giant hug. As she hugged me, my father came over and joined us for one of our famous family hugs. We stood there in silence for many minutes until my father said, "We best be going or you're going to miss the train, Ryko!"

On the way to the train station, my parents and I talked about my upcoming journey. Although there were very few plans or direction, which is normal for this journey, I did have some ideas. I told my parents how I wanted to take the train west and get off when it felt right. It may be a mile or a thousand.

My mother reminded me to mail postcards to keep them posted on my journey and where my travels took me. My father jokingly reminded me to stay away from white cats in alleyways in the city.

As we walked up to the train station, my mother handed me my backpack. She said, "I've packed you enough food for a couple of weeks, Ryko. And yes, even dessert." My mother's apple cake was the best of the best dessert any cat could ever ask for. I thanked her and told her a couple of weeks worth of her cake would be gone in an hour.

My father reached over and unzipped the front pocket of my backpack. He pulled out two books and said, "Ryko, here's your special journal. Be sure to note your thoughts, discoveries, and anything you find interesting. You'll be referring back to this your entire life so take great care of it. Also, I thought you may want to take this with you."

My father turned the other book around, and it was none other than *Whisker Hollow*.

We all walked arm-in-arm over to the ticket counter, I purchased my ticket, and as I turned around to look at my parents, we heard, "All aboard!"

My mother gave me another huge hug and looked deeply into my eyes and said, "Ryko, I love you so much, and I am so proud of you. You are going to have such an amazing journey. I know for sure you will."

My father put his arm around me and said, "Son, there is no prouder dad on this earth, and there never has been. I'm not only proud of you for who you are today, but I am even prouder of who you will become tomorrow. Always remember that. I love you."

I told my parents I loved them so much, thanked them for helping me prepare for my journey, and made my way to the train. As I stepped up onto the train, I looked back at my parents, let out a giant meow, and waved my paws.

I walked onto the train and found a seat by the window, so I could look out at my parents. I opened the window and said, "I'm sure I will be back before the snow falls. In fact, you can count on it! I love you both so much!"

The train started to move, and my journey began.

ENTRY 7

"Where you going, kid?" I must have dozed off. "I said, where you going, kid?" I opened my eyes and saw a much older cat than I, sitting across from me. He was either in his 9th life or very close to it. He was more gray and white than black, and his glasses were far too big for his face. He walked with a cane and held a briefcase on his lap.

I told him that I was just starting my journey, which I very soon regretted. For the next six hours, I heard every detail about his journey. How he had found his true love, how he learned to swim, and how he found his passion for singing. I literally did not say one single word during those six hours.

He was headed off to Chicago to visit his great-great grandcats that his 8th daughter just had. By this point, I was nearly headed off the train myself, through the window to escape.

I excused myself and walked to the snack bar to get some water. And my timing couldn't have been any better because the moment

I walked up to the counter, the cat at the counter placed a sign that read, "Sorry, out of water."

As I turned around to go find a new place to sit, another cat bumped into me and spilled her coffee all over me. Thankfully it was room temperature, but still. Being covered in coffee wasn't exactly on the list of ideal things that I wanted to experience on my journey. The other cat apologized up and down and helped dry me off with some napkins she had in her purse.

As I walked from railcar to railcar, I started to wonder if all of these things that happened were signs for me to get off the train. Maybe the universe was telling me that this was where I should get off the train and begin my journey?

I found a seat and curled up by the window as I watched the scenery pass by. I asked my heart if I should get off the train at the next stop, and I felt I should stay, even though my mind was telling me to get off as fast as possible. "Follow your heart, Ryko," I said to myself.

But you know, despite a little bit of a rough start, I was truly happy. I was so grateful to be starting my own journey and to find my path in life. I smiled as I drifted off to sleep.

ENTRY 8

SEVERAL UNEVENTFUL DAYS PASSED with the only excitement being that I was truly in awe of the scenery outside of the window. Then, one afternoon, I decided to grab my backpack and hop off the train at one of the stops.

Thinking back to that moment, there was literally no reason why I got off the train. I didn't think about it. I just stood up, walked off, and it just felt like the right thing to do. I guess you can say I was truly following my heart because the little voice in my head didn't tell me to stay on the train.

"Welcome to Austin, Texas!" a young cat yelled, as he was trying to sell newspapers to the other cats getting off the train.

A city. A real city! As I walked away from the train station, the hustle and bustle of the city soon surrounded me. Cats were coming and going. Some were enjoying organic milk in small milk shops, while others were listening to live music. There were cats lounging around under trees in a park. As I approached a river,

I could see dozens cf cats paddling around on what looked like stand-up surfboards.

I thought it looked like fun, so I decided to go down to the river and see if I could try stand-up surfing, too. After walking over to the river and around cats lounging around by the bank, I found a small stand with several surfboards in the water in front of it.

The worker asked me if I wanted to try it, and I excitedly said yes. Before I knew it I was already way down the river, having the time of my life. After a few hours, I became quite hungry but decided to save the food my mother gave me for a time when I didn't have any food available.

I paddled over to a fast cat food restaurant called Cat Food King to get something to eat. I walked inside and ordered a burger, fries, and some milk. Then I walked over to a table next to the windows and sat down.

As I sat eating my burger, a hippie-looking cat who worked there walked by me carrying a whole tray of burgers. Somehow he managed to trip and he fell flat on his face while a good twenty or more burgers went airborne and made one heck of a mess on the floor and wall of windows I was sitting next to.

I asked him if he was OK, and he got up laughing and said that was the third time today that had happened to him. I laughed and offered to help him clean up the mess, which he accepted very quickly.

"Name is Orky, what's your name?" The clumsy cat said.

"I'm Ryko," I told him, as I cleaned some pieces of burger off the wall. We talked for a few minutes while we cleaned up, and Orky invited me to hang out with him and some of his friends when he got out of work in a couple of hours. I accepted the invitation.

Once the mess was cleaned up, I left to go walk the banks of the river and take in some of the great Austin atmosphere. After a couple of hours of soaking it all in, I walked into the restaurant where Orky said to meet him. My nose quickly perked up, as the smell of sour milk filled the air.

I was offered some sour milk by one of the workers, but I denied it. I had never had sour milk before and just the smell of it made my stomach turn. How other cats were drinking it was beyond me.

I saw Orky sitting down at a table outside with some other cats and I walked over. "Ryko!" Orky yelled loud enough for the entire hill country to hear him. I smiled, walked over, and took a seat.

Orky asked what I was doing in Austin, and I told him that I was on my journey. He was really excited for me and told me about his journey, which he took just two years prior. Thankfully, his version was only about five minutes. Truthfully, I was still recovering from the six-hour marathon story from the cat on the train.

"So Orky, did you find out what your true passion is? Do you know your purpose in life?" I asked.

Orky looked at me with a big smile, and said, "Sure did buddy. I know exactly what it is. My journey provided a pretty clear path to what I'm supposed to be doing."

"Oh that is so good, Orky," I said. "Is it to work at Cat Food King?"

"No, no," Orky said while shaking his head and looking down at the ground. "It's definitely not working at Cat Food King. Sometimes life has other plans for you, even though you know what your true purpose is, I guess."

I was a bit confused because I had never heard of a cat learning what his purpose was and not following through with it. "So what is your calling then?" I asked Orky.

Orky took a deep breath and spoke softly. "As I was on my journey, I ended up walking through a giant field of catnip. I absolutely loved it there. In fact, I spent several days just rolling around in the catnip and having the best time of my life. One day, I saw the owner of the field harvesting the catnip, so I went up to him and talked to him about the business. To be honest, I fell in love with everything about it. At that moment I knew that I wanted to be a catnip farmer."

"So why are you not a catnip farmer, Orky?" I asked.

"Well, I don't know. It's just a lot of work, I guess. To be honest, sometimes it's easier to settle for what is, for lack of better words, easy than to go for what is hard and unknown. I normally would never admit this, but I am a scaredy-cat. I'm afraid that I will fail. And who wants to fail at something?" Orky said while looking down as his cup of sour milk. "So yeah, I settled. I get by. It's not the life I imagined for myself, but maybe I was just dreaming too big," Orky said.

I bent down so I could look Orky in the eyes. "You can never dream too big. In fact, you cannot dream big enough because whatever you dream can come true. Maybe it doesn't happen the way you imagined or as fast as you want it to. Maybe the work is much harder than you thought, but you can't give up. You should never give up on your dreams," I said.

Orky stood up from the table and looked at Ryko. "Yeah, I suppose you're right, Ryko. Hey, let me ask you, where did you learn to think and talk like that? I don't know if I've heard someone talk the way you do. It kind of lights a fire within me that I forgot all about. I used to have that fire, but I don't know where it went. I guess being a scaredy-cat puts the fire right out of me."

I thought about Orky's question for a moment. And the truth was, I didn't know where that came from. I've just always thought that way for as long as I can remember. I didn't know any different. "I guess from my parents?" I said.

Orky patted me on the shoulder. "Well, you're one lucky cat, Ryko. Hey, listen, I need to go help one of my buddies move into his new place, but I definitely want to keep in touch. I don't want to bother you on your journey and all, but maybe after we can hang out again sometime," Orky said.

"I'd love to," I said with a smile. I took out my journal and opened it. "Give me your address and I can write to you and we can arrange something," I told Orky. I gave him my notebook and he wrote down his address.

I put my journal back into my backpack and reached out my paw to shake Orky's paw. "It was truly a pleasure meeting you,

Orky, and don't let your fears get the best of you. Some of the most successful cats out there used to be scaredy cats, you know. I mean look at Sir Richard Catson."

Orky laughed. "I know, I know, Ryko. I'll work on it. I promise. Enjoy your journey, buddy. I look forward to hearing from you when you get back."

As I walked out of the restaurant, I stopped, took out my journal again and wrote the following under Orky's address:

No matter where my journey takes me, never give up on my dreams. Never forget who I truly am and who I wish to become. When I find and know my purpose, I must go after it. No matter what happens or doesn't happen. I must never settle for anything less. I am worth it. We are all worth it.

ENTRY 9

THE NEXT MORNING, I awoke from the cat bed I rented for the night and found out right away why the rooms were so cheap. As I opened my eyes, there were dozens of these super giant bugs crawling on the floor and wall. I had never seen such monsters. I promptly screamed like a kitten, loud enough to possibly shatter a window ten miles away.

I ran out of the room and up to the front desk to tell them about the monsters in my room that were surely trying to eat me. The cat at the desk laughed and said that they were called cockroaches and that it must be my first time in Texas. I slowly nodded my head as I backed up towards the exit. I considered that experience a real sign that time and headed back to the train station to continue heading west.

Once back on the train, I took a seat next to a window. After a few hours, low and behold, we were in West Texas. I looked out of the window, and it was like I was looking at a picture on the wall. I could tell we were moving, but the scenery just stayed the same for the longest time. I had never seen so much sand without the ocean.

I don't know about you, but seeing so much sand made me feel like I needed to pee. I couldn't tell you how many times I got up to use the litter box and nothing happened. Because the scenery out the window wasn't doing anything special, I kept myself busy walking around the rail cars, getting water, and taking naps. After some time passed, I looked out the window, and it was the same exact scene as it was hours earlier. I opened my backpack, took out my journal, and wrote:

Don't go back to West Texas, unless I need a never-ending supply of sand for the litterbox.

As I put my journal back into my backpack, I noticed a couple things. One, the food and desserts my mother made me. I decided it was time to eat a piece of cake. Okay, I ate four pieces of cake, but who's counting? And second, the *Whisker Hollows* book.

I decided to read my favorite for a while, and it wasn't long until I felt a tear running down my cheek. I sure did miss my mother and father and I felt bad. More than bad. Really guilty. I went to Austin and forgot to send them a postcard because I got so wrapped up in experiencing so many new things. I promised myself that the next time I got off the train that I'd mail them one. And then I ate more cake. Make that five pieces in total.

ENTRY 10

Unlike getting off the train in Austin, this time I got off the train with a purpose. Well, for two purposes. The first was that I really wanted to get a postcard to send to my parents. That was a priority. And second, when the train stopped in Denver I knew that I had to get off. I thought it would be funny to send my parents a postcard that said, "In Denver I stayed away from white cats in the alley like you said!"

Colorado had a very different feel than Texas. For one, the mountains in Colorado were nothing like I had ever seen in New Hampshire. They were so beautiful and absolutely ginormous. Second, the air was not nearly as thick. Honestly, the humidity was so high that I felt like I could jump up in the air in Texas and get stuck.

I walked around downtown Denver and walked into a gift shop. After searching through the postcards, I couldn't believe my eyes when I found one with a white cat sitting on a box with the city and mountains in the background. On the postcard it said, "DENVER" in big letters on the top, followed by "The mile-high city" below it. It was perfect.

I wrote my note to my parents and went to the counter. I paid for the postcard, postage, and mailed it off. I left the store with a giant smile. I remember thinking that I had wished I could see my parents' faces and hear their laughs when they got the postcard.

As I continued to walk, I found an amazing park that I thought would be great to relax in and do some cat watching. I walked over to a tree, took off my backpack, and sat down.

The weather was amazing and there were a lot of families in the park. Many were playing cat ball, some were having a picnic, and others were just laying down and enjoying the sun.

Although watching the families play together made me miss my parents, I felt like I was on top of the world. I was happy and I began to purr.

After maybe an hour of relaxing and enjoying the sights and sounds all around, a gray cat wearing a very worn jacket walked by me. I didn't think much about it at the time, but then I noticed he kept walking by me. Again and again. Each time he walked by, he walked a little slower and stared at me.

After about six times, he was pretty close to me, so I asked, "Excuse me, can I help you with something? Are you lost?" There was something about this cat that made me feel uneasy. I wasn't sure if I could trust him or if I was just being overly careful.

The gray cat stopped in his tracks and walked over to me quickly. I admit I was a little startled.

"Ah, hello there my good cat. Such a beautiful day to be at the park, isn't it?" the gray cat said as he sat down right in front of me.

"I suppose so, but may I ask, why do you keep walking past me?" I asked.

The gray cat looked on the ground all around him. "I was sitting right here earlier and lost my pocket watch. It must have fallen out of my pocket. You haven't seen it by any chance, have you? I mean, you didn't find it and steal it from me, right?"

"Oh no, I haven't seen it, and I most certainly would never steal your watch if I saw it on the ground. I'm sorry you lost it and am happy to help you look for it if you'd like," I said as I stood up and started looking.

After a few minutes of walking up and down the area between a few trees and a couple of benches, the gray cat leaned down to the ground. "I found it! Oh boy. My lucky pocket watch. Thank you for helping me look for it. Have a nice day my friend!" And the gray cat quickly ran off.

I thought I had walked by the exact area a dozen times where the gray cat found his watch. In fact, I know I did. It must have been a very small pocket watch because I certainly didn't see it on the ground. Or so I thought…

I walked back over to the tree that I had been sitting under and sat back down. I thought about the gray cat and how something didn't quite feel right about everything that just happened. I brushed it off because there was something else that was on my mind… Food!

This would be a perfect time to eat some lunch and maybe dessert. I reached over to where I put my backpack. Oh. My. God.

My backpack was gone.

I jumped up and ran around the tree. It wasn't there.

I ran up to a couple of cats who were walking by and asked if they had seen it. They hadn't.

I ran over to a couple of kittens playing cat ball and asked them if they saw my backpack.

They did not.

At this point, I was frantic. I ran all around the park asking everyone I saw if they had seen my backpack.

Not a single cat had seen it.

I walked over to a bench, sat down, and cried. How could someone steal my backpack? What about my food? What about my journal? What about the *Whisker Hollows* book?

To say the least, I was beyond devastated.

Of course, I was upset about not having the food my mother had packed me. And yes, losing my *Whisker Hollows* book was beyond painful. I'll probably never find another one. But my journal. The journal my parents gave me to document my journey. There's no way that I will ever remember everything I had already written down.

I began to cry harder. As I let out a giant meow, I felt a tap on my shoulder.

I looked up and saw a police cat. "Are you okay, son?" The officer asked.

"No. Someone stole my backpack from under the tree. It had everything in it. Food, my favorite book, and my journal," I said, as I wiped away a few tears.

"Oh no. Not another one. Did someone tell you that they lost their keys?" the officer asked.

"No, a gray cat in an old worn jacket had lost his watch and I tried to help him," I said.

"I am so sorry this happened," the officer said. "But that is why they have me working in the park this weekend. There are a few cats going around telling others they lost something on the ground and when a cat helps them look for the lost possession, another cat runs up and steals their belongings. They work as a team."

I couldn't even say a word. I had never had anyone steal from me. I felt feelings I had never felt before. And I just shook my head because I felt my parents would be so disappointed in me. After all, what were the odds that years ago, my father almost had his backpack stolen in Denver on his journey, and now I'm here, and my backpack is gone?

"Look, there's a chance, and I mean a very, very small chance you can get your stuff back," the officer said.

I leaped up from the bench. "How? Please tell me. I'll do anything," I cried.

"The only reason why these two cats are stealing things is to sell them to make money. After they steal things, they go around to the local resale shops and try to sell them. We've been trying to catch these cats for the past two weeks, and it hasn't been easy. We tried to catch one at a resale shop across the street last weekend, but he got away."

"This is great news!" I said. "Please tell me how to get to the resale shop. Which way do I go?"

The officer looked at me and frowned. "Son, there are fifty-nine resale shops in the city of Denver. As I said, it's a very small chance. I'm so sorry this happened, and I wish you luck finding your things."

As the officer walked away, I just stood there. Fifty-nine resale shops? That is going to take me a week or more to go to all of them. By that time, my things will probably be gone.

I sat back down on the bench, and for the first time on my journey, I was considering just going back home. Maybe I wasn't ready to go on my journey after all. Maybe this was a sign that I needed to try again next year. Or maybe, just maybe I was being tested.

Suddenly, I felt a rush of energy down my spine that made the hair on the back of my neck puff up. It puffed up so much that a woman walking by me must have thought I was up to no good, and hissed at me.

"I'm so sorry, ma'am," I said. She turned around and growled at me. Jeesh. I guess she was having a bad day too.

I thought for a moment. "Yes. That's it, I'm being tested," I said to myself. "This is one of those lessons that I need to figure out the hard way." I leaped to my feet, started walking, and began working on my master plan to get my backpack and all my things back.

ENTRY 11

IT TOOK NEARLY TWO HOURS to make little red dots all over the map. But now, laying on the ground in front of me was a map of Denver showing the exact location of each and every resale shop that I found in the phone book.

As I looked at the map, I thought about the gray cat and his stealing friend. If I'm going to find my backpack, I need to think like bad cats. If I were one, what would I do? Where would I take the backpack to sell it? I thought and thought.

Now, the bad cats obviously know that the police are onto them because they were chased from a resale shop across the street from the park recently.

So there was no way they were going to any resale shop anywhere near the park, I thought. They would have to go far away to make sure that they didn't get caught selling stolen goods.

And that's what I based my entire plan on. To start going to every resale shop around, starting with the furthest one outside of Denver and work my way towards the park. There wasn't any other choice.

I walked into the first resale shop on the list, which was called, *Whisker Resale Shop.* I walked inside and over to the counter where there was a cat working. I asked if anyone had stopped by to try to sell a backpack that had food, a book, and a journal inside. I was told no and the cat spent ten minutes trying to sell me another backpack. I refused.

I walked to the next resale shop, The Paw and Jewel Shop. I walked in and was greeted by a very nice cat. I told him what had happened and asked if anyone had come in the store with my backpack. Sadly, the answer was no.

This process continued for the rest of the day until I couldn't take another step. My paws were hurting from all the walking. In total, I had stopped at sixteen resale shops and had nothing to show for it besides the pads on my paws aching so badly.

I decided to call it a night. I hobbled over to a hotel and rented a cat bed for the night. And yes, I was assured there were no Texas monsters that would try to eat me.

I awoke the next morning and quickly hit the road. I walked into Cash N Paws on Federal Boulevard. There was a cat in front of me at the counter, so I had to wait several minutes. He was trying to sell his collar that he insisted was diamond-studded, but the resale shop owner tested the diamonds and said that they were fake.

The cat left very angry and I walked up to the counter. "Excuse me," I asked. "Has anyone come in to sell a backpack filled with food, a book, and a journal?"

"Yes, someone did last night," the cat at the counter said to me, as he focused on the crossword puzzle he was working on.

"What?" I leaped up and down. "Do you have it? It is mine. It was stolen from me yesterday!" I could barely contain myself.

The resale shop owner looked up at me and said, "No, I'm sorry, I don't. I passed on buying it. They were asking way too much money for it, so I told them to move along."

My heart sank to the floor for a moment, but then I became excited as I yelled, "OK, thank you!" and I ran out the door.

My adrenaline was pumping, and the hairs on my back started to stand up. I quickly opened the map and drew a big circle around the Cash N Paws shop and noted that there were 5 other resale shops very close by.

I ran to the first one, which was literally across the street, and the door was locked. I looked up at the door and noticed a sign that said, "Family emergency. Be back on Tuesday." I made a note on my map and went to the next one, which was just a few minutes down the road.

I ran in and asked the owner of the resale shop about my backpack. She said that no one had been in there trying to sell a backpack and noted that no one had actually come in for the past three days. She then started telling me stories about her 23 grandkittens, and wanted to show me photos of all of them. I felt bad, but I had to tell her I was in a hurry and quickly left.

The next resale shop on my list was a couple miles away, so I decided to walk and save my energy.

I reached Fast Cash Resale Shop, walked in, and walked up to the counter. "Excuse me," I said to the cat who had his nose in a book. After a few seconds, I said, "Hello?" Still no response.

I noticed a bell sitting on the top of the counter. I tapped it with my paw and it made a ding-ding-ding sound a few times. Finally, the cat behind the counter lifted his nose from the book he was reading, stood up, and said, "Sorry, how can I help you?"

"Has anyone come by trying to sell a backpack?" I asked, rather frantically.

The cat leaned in a little closer to me, pushed his glasses closer to his face, and asked, "Who wants to know?"

"Well I do, of course," I said. "I had my backpack stolen from me yesterday, and I've been going to every resale shop around Denver ever since. I have to find it."

The cat slowly turned around, walked over to the desk, and

picked up a notebook. "I had the day off yesterday. Let me see what items Lucy bought. She's a crazy cat, you know. She buys everything. We keep telling her not to but she just believes every story that comes in here."

I tried to peek over his shoulder to see if I could see what items were written down in the notebook, but everything was written in this strange writing style called cursive. Apparently that writing style must be some secret language because most of us millennicats can't read it.

The resale shop cat walked over to the counter. "OK, yes. I see she did purchase a backpack yesterday. It looks like it contained a couple of books and food. Is that the one?"

I literally jumped up in the air and screamed, "YES! That is my backpack! Please, can I have it? Where is it?"

It seemed my energy startled him a little, as he took a couple steps back from me and said, "Look, it's in processing right now. The owner of the shop needs to go through everything we bring in so he can price it. I'm not allowed to."

A few tears welled up in my eyes. "Please," I said as I tried to compose myself. "I'm on my journey. That backpack was given to me by parents and contains food my mother made for me, the journal they gave me, and my favorite book. I'll give you anything for it. Please."

"I see," he said. "I also did my own journey a year or so back. And honestly, I don't know what I would have done if I had lost my journal, besides somehow preventing my parents from killing me. Let me go out back and see if I can find it. I'll be right back."

"My name is Ryko. It says Ryko on the side of the backpack," I yelled.

What felt like an eternity passed, and the resale shop worker walked back to the counter. "Is this it?"

"YES!" I screamed and went to grab my backpack, but he pulled it back.

He then walked over to the small desk against the wall back behind the counter. "I need to call my boss and explain the situation.

Like I said, I'm not allowed to give or sell things back you know. We are a resale shop. We are in business to sell stuff and make money," he said, as he picked up the phone and started to dial.

"Wait. Please. Listen. What's your name?" I asked.

"My name is Roky. Why?"

I took a deep breath.

"Roky, hold on a second here, let me ask you something. When you took your journey, what did you find? Did you find your calling?"

Roky stopped dialing the phone and slowly hung it up. He walked over to the counter and looked at me. "Yes, but I had always sort of known. It was just confirmed. And, well, it's complicated."

"What do you mean? Finding one's path is usually the complicated part, but once you know which path to take, then it's easy, they say. You just walk down the path you were meant to walk on," I said.

Roky walked away from around the counter and sat on an old green chair that had so much cat hair on it, it could almost pass for a new type of animal.

"Have a seat, Ryko. Since you are on your own journey, let me share something with you that I wish I had known while I was on my journey."

I walked over to the chair next to Roky and was startled by the amount of hair on that chair, too. It had even more hair than the green chair, and I wasn't sure if the chair was going to bark, meow, or what. I took a chance, sat down, and was surprised at how comfortable the chair was.

"What is it?" I asked.

"Take your time. Really. Don't rush it. Enjoy the journey. Soak it all in. Don't rush to get back like I did," Roky said, as he took off his thick glasses to clean them.

"Why did you rush your journey?" I asked.

Roky put his glasses back on and took a deep breath. "Parents. I mean who do you think of when you think of the name, Roky? A scrapping fighter cat or some sports superstar?"

"A scrapping fighter cat?" I answered.

Roky shook his head. "You see, my parents named me Roky because they decided to name me after my father. They thought that I would have all the same skills he has. After all, my father holds the record for the number of trophies won by any cat in all of Colorado. He was the best cat at every sport he played, and he played them all. Heck, he still plays bat-a-ball a few times a week and is still the best in Denver."

"Oh that is exciting! Do you have all the skills your father has?" I asked.

"Are you kidding?" Roky said, as he licked his paw and rubbed his ear. "Ever since I was a kitten, my parents wanted me to play sports. They put me in everything and I was the worst cat on the team. On every team. I couldn't stand sports, but I also couldn't stand my parents not being as nice to me if I said I didn't want to play. I was stuck. So I just kept playing, even though I hated every second of it."

"I see," I said. "How did you end up working here then?"

"Well, before I left on my journey, my parents told me to be back in three weeks because there was a bat-a-ball tournament they said I had to be at. I didn't care so much about the journey because I had already figured out what I wanted to do. I just didn't know how I was going to break the news to my parents. Honestly, I was more excited about having three weeks of not being forced to play sports and finally getting some alone time to read."

Roky looked over at a box of cat balls. He reached in, grabbed one, and threw it across the room and hit a poster of Kitty Perry that was hanging on the wall next to a window. I didn't move. I really didn't know what to say.

After a moment of silence, Roky continued. "The night I left on my journey I packed as many books I could fit into a giant backpack and hid it in the woods behind the house. When it was time for me to go the next morning, I said goodbye to my parents, who, of course, made me promise I would be back in time for my game.

I left, then snuck around the back and changed the backpack they gave me with the one I prepared. I walked for an hour, found a tree I could climb up, and that's where I spent my three weeks."

I looked over at Roky. "Oh wow, I'm so sorry. I can't even imagine what that was like."

"It was freaking amazing!" Roky said with a huge smile. "I got to do exactly what I love to do: Read. I love reading. I read all the books I took with me three times. I also love math. And if you haven't noticed, I wear glasses. So Rkyo, I'm a nerd, and I'm very proud of it. A nerd that doesn't like and is really horrible at sports. Believe it or not, when I threw the ball, I was actually aiming at the window, and not the poster. Yes, I'm that bad."

We both shared a good laugh.

"Look Ryko. All I want to do is read books about history, science, math, and learn about logistics. I love logistics. Back a couple of months ago, my parents and I had a falling out. I couldn't take one more day of being forced to do something that I had no interest in, so I moved in with my friend and got this job because the library isn't hiring right now. I get to read almost all day long and teach myself logistics while being here. Plus, I get to see new books that come into the resale shop every day, so it's all good, besides the part about my parents. They are really disappointed in me for not being the sports superstar that they always wanted me to be."

Roky got up and walked over to the counter, took out a piece of paper, and wrote something down. I was still trying to figure out what the word logistics meant. Huh. New one for me.

"I really don't know what it's like to have a family that doesn't support my dreams. I can't imagine what that would be like for a minute, let alone your whole life. I'm really sorry, Roky. But I am happy you are working towards doing what you love, and I really hope that you and your parents can make up real soon," I said.

Roky grabbed my backpack, walked back over to the green chair, and sat down. "Well, I'm doing what I really like right now, but I know one day I'll be doing what I love. My future is in logistics.

That's the future of the world, you know. By the way, you said you have your favorite book in your backpack. That was honestly all I heard when you said what was in there," he said, laughing.

"Oh, that book is my favorite story in the world. It means so much to me. And I've heard that there is an even crazier back story to the book. I don't think that there are many left out there," I said.

Roky became lit up in a way I didn't think was even possible for his type. "Wait, you are telling me, right here and now, that you have a rare book in your backpack? This is like the best day ever! You have no idea how awesome this is. Look, I'm a book nerd, and I absolutely live for moments like this."

The poor cat was literally trembling with excitement.

Roky looked down at my backpack. "I'm not one to ever break rules, you know. I'm a nerdy rule follower and proud of it, but I like you, Ryko. You're a really cool cat. So I wrote Lucy a note she'll see when she comes in tomorrow and let her know the person who she bought the backpack from made a mistake and picked it back up. It's a little white lie, but I don't see any harm in it."

"Roky, thank you so much," I said softly.

"But there's only one condition," Roky looked up at me.

"What's that?" I asked.

"You absolutely must show me this rare book that you have in your backpack. I don't know how much longer I can hold out!" Roky said laughing, and still slightly trembling. "Here, take your backpack and let's see this book of yours."

Roky handed me the backpack and I gave it a huge hug. I opened up the zipper and was surprised that everything was still inside. The cats who stole my backpack had no idea what they were missing. I was fully expecting my food, especially the apple cake dessert to be gone.

"Before I show you the book, you have to try this cake that my mother made. It's seriously the best cake ever."

I handed Roky a piece of the cake, and he took one bite, and then ate the whole thing in his next bite.

"That was in your backpack, too? It's probably a good thing I didn't know. All that cake would have been long gone by now. It is delicious! Can I have just one more piece?"

I took out another piece of cake for Roky and slid my *Whisker Hollows* book out of my backpack and held it up for him to see. What happened next, I'll never forget and is probably something I never want to see again.

Literally, the second Roky's eyes hit the *Whisker Hollows* book, he became so excited, he peed. And not a little dribble or a few drops. I mean like straight up peed.

Roky jumped up from the chair. "OK, look. First, I'm sorry. I sometimes pee when I get overly excited. You should see me at a spelling bee or algebra competition. Second, I cannot believe my eyes right now. Do you have any idea what you have in your hands? This is unbelievable. Can I hold it, please?"

I handed the *Whisker Hollows* book over to Roky. He quickly and carefully placed it in his lap and put on some white gloves.

"A book like this is so rare and valuable, you can never be too careful," Roky said as he slowly opened the book and turned through the first few pages.

"You know, book collectors stopped trying to find this book. There was an article a few years ago that talked about how this was a lost treasure, gone forever. All the books were either long gone or everyone mailed them back to the publisher many years ago."

I looked over to see what page Roky was on. "Oh yes, I know the story. I don't know how my parents ended up with the book. But it's one that speaks to me more than any other book I've read. In fact, I've memorized the poem in the back and think about it often."

"Poem?" Roky carefully turned to the last page of the book. "Ah yes. This is what many had thought held clues on how to find Whisker Hollows. Cats went pretty crazy over this many years ago, you know."

I leaned back into my furry chair. "Oh yes, I've heard the stories, but Whisker Hollows was never found. Or at least if someone did find it, they didn't tell anyone. But who knows, maybe it's all just a story. That's one of many things that I love about it. It's a story that you just don't really know if it's real or not. It sounds real. It feels real. York did an amazing job at describing Whisker Hollows."

Roky closed the book and looked over at me. "You know Ryko, there are many, many cats who would pay you an absolute fortune for this book. You would never have to work a day in your life. Or, you could let the media know you own a copy and you'd be the most famous cat in the world. Seriously. This is huge."

I laughed. "Roky, I highly doubt all of that. But what I don't doubt is that *Whisker Hollows* has shaped me into who I am today and is shaping me into who I will become tomorrow. And that, my friend, no amount of money or fame could ever buy."

I looked over at Roky, and he was frozen. I'm not sure if he was in shock or about to pee again or what. He was a cool cat, just a little different than other cats you could say.

It was getting dark and it was already an hour past closing time. We both stood up and I put my backpack on.

"Well Ryko, it has been an absolute pleasure meeting you, sir. I trust you will have the most fabulous journey, and you will no doubt find your true purpose," Roky said, as he extended his paw for a shake.

I reached out to his paw and gave it a good, firm shake. "Thank you, Roky. I don't know how I will ever repay you, but I promise, I'm going to come up with something. Here, please write your address in my journal. I'll be back in touch when I return home."

Roky wrote down his address and I walked out of the resale shop a very happy, thankful, and grateful cat.

I walked to a nearby hotel, which I made sure was Texas monster-free. Before calling it a night, I took out my journal and made an entry.

If something or someone doesn't feel or seem right, trust that feeling.

A journey can be made short by living someone else's dreams for you and not your own.

Some cats can come into your life and turn an upside-down world right side up in a blink of an eye.

Consider not sharing so much cake next time.

ENTRY 12

I ONLY HAD ONE THING on my mind when I woke up the next morning: Leave Denver. Although I had a quite unfortunate experience with my backpack getting stolen, I was very grateful for meeting Roky. I also really loved the city and all of the cats there. Certainly, one bad experience isn't the city's fault. I'd love to come back someday.

I made my way to the train station and hopped on the first train out of Denver. I didn't even notice what direction it was going or even where it was going. It was just time for me to continue my journey.

While on the train, I opened my backpack to take out my *Whisker Hollows* book to read it. And it was gone.

Roky stole it.

I'm only kidding. I had the book in my hands. I had you there for a minute, right?

I opened the book in my lap, and after just a few minutes, I drifted off to sleep.

Suddenly, I was jolted awake by the sound of cats cheering and a lot of movement around the train. A moment later, an overly loud announcement was made on the speakers that said, "Welcome to Las Vegas, kitties!"

Las Vegas. The city of lights. Maybe it was all the lights. Or the sounds. Or just the sheer excitement in the air. Whatever it was, it drew me in like a moth to a lightbulb at night.

Walking around Las Vegas at night was quite an experience. I ended up filling my backpack with an untold number of cards that nice cats were handing out on the street. Once I realized what was on those cards, I quickly filled up a nearby trash can.

After countless hours of walking up and down the Las Vegas Strip, as they called it, I headed back to the train station to continue my journey. I thought about mailing my parents a postcard, but I decided to wait until the next stop. Hopefully I would have something exciting to share then.

Across the street from the train station, there was a small cat ball field, with a lot of cats playing and many times more cheering the players on. Since I had an hour to wait until the next train, I decided to walk over and watch the game.

I entered the fenced-off area and found a single open seat down on the first row. I had never seen a crowd so excited about a game, but it didn't take me long to realize that they weren't all there for the game per se. They were there to watch one player in particular and he was pretty easy to spot out.

Kyro had on a bright lime green headband and matching shirt with his name in huge letters on the front and back. It was the same shirt that nearly half of the audience was wearing, the same audience who would cheer Kyro's every move.

Now I must admit, I had never ever seen any cat play cat ball at the level Kyro was playing. Watching him play was like watching a legend whose stories were larger than real life, except Kyro was performing his legendary skills right there in front of everyone. I was in awe.

When Kyro had the ball, you could see the look of disappointment spread across the faces of all the players on the other team. There was just no touching him. Kyro had moves that he had created on his own, and apparently, he not only named all of them, but he would announce loudly to the audience which move he was about to make.

"Here's my One-Two Left-Right Swoosheroo Tap-in" he yelled, as he performed the moves so quickly that even watching in slow motion, you'd miss half of the moves his paws made. Within seconds, he was already down the other side of the field.

All the other cats who were chasing him, trying to get the ball, were now all on the ground dizzy from running around in circles. And I admit, I was just as dizzy watching Kyro's blazing speed moves from the stands.

Boom! A firework went off, and lights flashed from the goal as Kyro scored his 17th goal for the game. Now keep in mind, in a normal game of cat ball, you rarely ever see more than five goals. Heck, the most I ever scored, playing with my father and with friends, was two. And I thought that I was pretty good and had some moves.

"Look at me now!" Kyro yelled as he tapped the ball with his right paw, ran in a circle around someone on the other team, hit the ball again with his tail, and then shot the ball into the goal with his head. Watching this cat was just unbelievable. Unheard of. I just didn't understand why he wasn't playing professional ball. He'd surely be the most famous cat ball player in the U.S., probably even the world.

After the game, Kyro came up to the stands to sign autographs. People had posters of Kyro, shirts, headbands, and jerseys, all getting signed. After each signature, Kyro would yell, "Who's the greatest cat ball player in town?" And the crowd would follow, "Kyro, Kyro. He's the best one around!"

When Kyro got near me, I unzipped my backpack and took out my journal. I figured I might as well get Kyro to sign a page. He will surely become a famous cat ball player soon.

As Kyro approached my section, you could literally feel his high energy, everyone in the stands fed off of it. Between yelling and signing autographs, Kyro was sure to take a few seconds to talk to every single cat who he signed something for, especially the kittens.

As he approached my section, I overheard one of his interactions with a kitten in front of me. "How's it going little buddy?" Kyro asked as he signed the kitten's poster. The kitten just looked up at Kyro with his giant eyes and had a big smile on his face.

"What do you want to be when you grow up?" Kyro asked.

The kitten replied, "I want to be a spacecat!"

Kyro leaned in towards the kitten, looked him right in the eyes and said, "Little buddy, you can literally be anything you set your mind to. Just stay focused, work hard, and keep that dream alive. I think you're going to be the best spacecat this world has ever seen!"

Kyro gave a big high five to the kitten and then walked over to me. I handed my journal and pen to him.

"Hey buddy, how are you this evening?" Kyro asked as he saw my journal and paused for a moment as he looked at it.

"I'm doing amazing. Great game tonight, sir!" I said, with a big smile.

"Thanks! That's so great to hear. Quick question. Is this your journey journal?" Kyro asked me.

"Yes, it is," I responded.

"Oh, that is so awesome. You must be coming to my event tonight. I can't wait to see you there!" Kyro said as he signed a page in my journal.

I watched him write something in my journal and sign his name. "I'm so sorry, I don't know about your event tonight. I'm just passing through Las Vegas."

Kyro finished writing and closed the book. "You have to come tonight. I host a monthly seminar for cats who are on their journey. Here, have this." He reached into his pocket, pulled out a ticket and handed it to me, along with my journal and pen.

As I looked down at the ticket, Kyro moved on to continue signing autographs.

The ticket said:
How To Have The Best Journey Ever
Presenter: Kyro
Location: CAT Studios Hotel
Conference Room: 1223
When: Tonight 9 PM
Admit: 1

I walked down from the stands and back onto the street to get away from the hustle and bustle of the crowd. I still had my journal in my hand and decided to open it and see what Kyro wrote. It said:

Work hard. You got this! You will be a champion! - Kyro

I put my journal back into my backpack and looked at the ticket. Then I looked at the train station. Then back down at my ticket. Since I didn't have any idea of where my journey was taking me next, I decided to go to Kyro's seminar to see what it was all about. It was starting in just a couple of hours, so I had plenty of time to walk there.

ENTRY 13

CATS, CATS, AND MORE CATS. Cats were everywhere. It was at that exact moment that I realized I'm not one for large crowds. But, I couldn't help but be attracted to the buzz and energy in the air.

As I walked towards conference room 1223, there were large banners of Kyro hanging on the wall that had a picture of him wearing a suit, smiling and pointing his paw forward. In big letters on the top, it says, "KYRO," And below his name, it read, "To be the best, learn from the best."

I couldn't help but let out a little smirk. It was obvious between the game of cat ball I watched earlier and seeing these posters that Kyro may be a little too full of himself. But from what I saw of Kyro thus far, he was the best at cat ball, so he was telling the truth.

As I walked into the conference room, the energy level was even higher. Dance music was playing loudly over the speakers, different colored lights were shining all around, and cats were dancing all over the place.

I worked my way up towards the stage and found an empty seat seven rows back from the front. I sat down as the cat sitting next to me jumped up on her chair and started to dance with the cat next to her. I just sat there, soaking it all in. Besides, I could not dance to save my life.

Suddenly the music stopped and all the lights went out except one bright spotlight that was focused onto a single point on the stage floor.

Music began to fill the conference room again, but this time it was much more dramatic music, like what you'd hear if a warrior cat was preparing for battle.

Then, a giant shadow appeared in the background, and the crowd went wild. Kyro slowly walked up to the circle of light cast onto the floor and the crowd went totally ballistic. The cheering was so loud that I actually had to cover my ears.

Kyro was wearing a dark gray suit, just like what he was wearing on in the posters. He had on a bright green tie, shiny shoes, and looked really sharp. I was surprised to see he was still wearing his bright green headband as well. Granted, it was obviously a new one as the one he wore earlier was drenched in sweat.

Kyro stood there for nearly three minutes while the crowd cheered and then held out both paws to the audience. Within seconds, it was completely silent in the conference room.

He slowly lowered his paws and just stood there silently.

Ten seconds passed. Then thirty. Then an entire minute. Kyro just stood there, looking straight ahead. His eyes were intensely focused. I allowed my eyes to wander around at some of the cats around me. There was such anticipation building and I started to squirm around in my seat a little. I looked around to see if other cats were doing the same thing. They were.

Then Kyro began.

"Focus. Determination. Drive. Desire. Purpose. Tenacity. Motivation. Urgency." Kyro paused, and took one step forward. "You are here today because you are on your journey. Who here wants to find their true purpose?" The crowd went wild.

"Who here wants to find their mission?" The crowd went crazy.

"Who here wants to be the very best that they can be?" The crowd lost it.

"Who here wants to discover the exact steps you need to take to literally guarantee you will find your exact purpose in your journey?" The crowd started jumping and screaming.

"And who here wants to... WIN?" The crowd basically peed themselves. I did not, but I almost did.

OK, I will admit it. Maybe just one drop escaped. But really, only one drop.

Kyro slowly walked over to the left side of the stage. "Your journey does not define who you will become. Your journey simply proves who you already are. You need to stop questioning it. Stop fighting it and start living today as the cat you envision yourself being tomorrow."

Nearly every cat around me had their journals out, taking notes at a rapid pace. I decided to open my backpack and get my journal out and start writing things down, too.

"I did not become the top ranked cat ball player in Las Vegas without a winning plan. I did not become the #1 sales rep for Hiss Cat Toys in Las Vegas without a winning plan. I did not become the #1 sales manager in the country without a winning plan. And I did not become the #1 motivational journey speaker in the country without a winning plan. Do you see the common thread here?"

The crowd all yelled out, "A winning plan!"

Kyro bent his knees, jumped up, and said, "Exactly! You have to have a winning plan in life. If you are not planning out your own winning life, guess what happens, my fellow winning cats? There is another cat that will plan your life for you. And let me tell you something, their plan is about them winning, not you. So remember that. You have to have a winning plan in life."

As Kyro spoke, I could feel a little spark and a small flame start to burn inside of me. I wrote notes down as quickly as I could in my journal. Although I wasn't on board with Kyro being so full of himself, he certainly did have some good pieces of advice.

For nearly two hours, Kyro shared ideas and tips on how cats could make the most out of their journey. I took fourteen pages of notes. Granted, looking at them now, I can only read about four of those pages. Between the dark room and writing as fast as I could, my handwriting looked more like cat scratch.

At the end of the seminar, Kyro then invited everyone to join his Cattermind program, for a special, one-time limited offer, only available for that evening. Even though it was a really good deal, it was still far too pricey for my budget. I passed.

Kyro walked off the stage to a standing ovation, and the lights came back on. Half the cats ran to the back of the room to sign up for Kyro's Cattermind program. I slowly made my way towards the doors and chatted with a few other cats as we walked out.

Once I got out of the conference room, I noticed several booths set up outside selling various items. I decided to go take a look to see what items were for sale.

The selection of products Kyro had was truly impressive. He had posters, his cat ball jerseys, headbands, booklets, tons of cat toys, pens, journals, and dozens of other products. I did end up buying a lime green headband that said "PLAN TO WIN" on it. Don't judge. I was caught up in the moment, okay?

I spent another hour in the halls chatting with other cats, who were all on various stages of their journey. Some were about to begin, some were in the middle, and some had recently finished their journeys.

It was getting late, so I excused myself from a conversation and headed towards the door to leave the hotel. Well, what I thought was the door to leave the hotel anyway. I didn't realize that Kyro's posters were blocking the signs on how to exit the maze of hallways that seemed to go on forever.

I took one turn after another through a series of hallways and reached the end of a hallway that had a single door at the end. I opened the door and saw that it was a parking garage. I figured that I might as well continue to go out that way. Surely a parking garage would lead me back to the street.

I was surprised that the garage was almost completely empty, besides a single car parked by an elevator that said "Employees Only" above it. But this wasn't just any car. This was the most expensive car a cat could buy. In fact, I had a poster of this car in my room growing up.

It was a two-toned, light and dark blue Catley. The fastest street-legal car ever made. Most cats do not earn enough in a lifetime to afford one of these cars. And I had never seen one in real life. I slowly walked up to it as I admired its absolute beauty.

The pictures of this car didn't do it justice. Seeing it in real life was an experience that is impossible to describe with words. You don't just look at the Catley, you feel it.

As I walked around to look at the front of the car, I heard the elevator coming and panicked. I didn't know what to do or where to go. I had a feeling I probably wasn't supposed to be there, and I certainly didn't want to get in trouble.

I ran over back to the door that I came from and it was locked. Oh no.

I looked around and there was absolutely no place to hide, so I did what any other cat would do in this situation. I put my backpack down, sat down, and started to lick myself.

Even though I heard the loud "ding" from the elevator, I didn't dare look up. I just continued to clean myself like there was no tomorrow. I was so nervous that I was licking myself about ten times faster than any cat would normally do. I imagine if anyone saw me, they'd think I looked ridiculous.

Suddenly, I heard the elevator doors open. My tongue was going about 60 licks per minute. Then I heard footsteps. The speed increased to at least 120 licks per minute. And then the footsteps were getting louder as they approached me. My tongue peaked at nearly 200 licks per minute and then failed.

"You OK?" I heard a voice ask.

I looked up and could feel my tongue hanging out of my mouth, but it was completely numb.

"Yessssh, bime obay," I sort of said.

The cat standing in front of me came into vision as my eyes adjusted to the light after keeping them squeezed shut during my panic licking attack.

I just looked at him while I reached up to my tongue and put it back in my mouth. It was him.

It was Kyro.

ENTRY 14

"WHAT DID YOU THINK?" Kyro asked.

"Huh?" I said, as I continued to get my bearings.

Kyro pointed to the headband laying on the ground by my backpack. I forgot to zip my backpack after I purchased it and it fell out when I put my backpack down in a panic.

"Oh, it was so amazing, sir. I took a ton of notes. I'm on my journey and this was perfect timing. I'm just really excited to be here, I mean to go there, I mean to the seminar, and I…"

Kyro extended his paw, "Relax little buddy. It's all good. Hey, wait a minute. You are the cat that was at my cat ball game earlier. The one I gave a ticket to, right?"

I grabbed Kyro's paw and he pulled me up. "Yes, sir. That was me. Well, that is me. I'm Ryko."

"Well Ryko, you're not really supposed to be in this garage, you know. What are you doing here?" Kyro asked.

"I got lost and the door that I came in through is locked. I'm a bit stuck in this garage," I said as I picked up the headband, put it in my backpack, and zipped it up.

"Well, no worries little buddy, let's get you out of here." Kyro turned around and started walking towards the Catley. I just stood there, frozen.

"Hop in." Kyro walked over to the Catley and opened the driver's side door. "I'll get you out of here."

My mind was racing as I walked towards the car. I couldn't believe this. I was about to sit inside a Catley! It's going to be nearly impossible for anything to top this on my journey. Just wait until my father and mother hear about this!

I walked over to the passenger side, opened the door, and got in. The only thing inside that made it look like a car was the steering wheel. Besides that, with all the lights and amazingly sleek design, I would have thought I was sitting in some sort of spaceship. It was more amazing than any picture I had ever seen.

"I must say, sir…"

"Kyro. Call me Kyro, Ryko," Kyro said as he put his seatbelt on.

"I must say, Kyro, this is the most beautiful car I have ever seen. I have a poster of this exact same car in my room. It's so amazing," I said as I looked all around me in disbelief that this was actually happening.

"That's funny!" Kyro said laughing. "I had a poster of this exact car in my room too. And I knew with all of my heart that someday I would have one. I knew it. Do you know how, Ryko?"

"Because you…" I started to say.

"WINNING!" Kyro said loudly as I jumped so dramatically that if I didn't have my seatbelt on, I would have ejected myself out of the car.

"I'm a champion. I work hard. I play hard. If I want something, I work for it. That's what champions do," Kyro said sternly.

"Are you a champion, Ryko?" Kyro asked as he started his beast of a car.

Embarrassingly, the vibration and rumble of the powerful engine and exhaust made me start to purr. I struggled to contain myself.

"I… I'm working on it. Well, I am. But it's a little different. I know with all my heart that I am here for a huge purpose. I've felt it all my life. I'm just still processing everything tonight. This way of thinking is all so new to me," I said slowly, as I tried to find the words.

Kyro paused before he let his foot off the brake to back out of the parking spot. "It's easy Ryko. You just look at yourself in the mirror, look into your own eyes, and tell yourself that you are a champion and that you will do whatever it takes. You do that enough, you start to not only believe it, but you act it. You are a champion, Ryko. Everyone is. Unfortunately, most don't know it or believe it."

I thought about what Kyro said for a moment as we backed out of the parking space. I had so many questions, so many things I wanted to say. I was worried though. I probably only had one minute at the most before we got back out onto the street and I was out of the car.

I needed to quickly think about what questions I wanted to ask. Obviously, Kyro had everything figured out and was doing quite well for himself.

"So Kyro," I began, "You are by far the best cat ball player I have ever seen. You are even better than the pro cat ball players. Probably even all of them. Why aren't you playing cat ball professionally?"

Kyro stayed silent and continued driving slowly down the ramp in the parking garage for a few seconds, and then we came to a stop.

"It's the one thing that got away from me," Kyro said as he slowly nodded his head, looking straight ahead.

"It's not really something I talk about much. Really, I never talk about it. But I had a shot. Heck, I was even offered a contract to play pro ball. But I made some bad choices during that time, Ryko. I let it all go to my head. Long story short, I blew it, kid."

I looked over at Kyro and asked, "Blew what? The opportunity to play pro cat ball?"

"That and a lot of other things. Sour milk can bring out the best and worst of cats, you know. And for me, it was the worst. I haven't touched the stuff since..." Kryo looked off into the distance. He had a look on his face I had not seen him make.

"Look, Ryko. You seem like a sharp cat. I don't know where you are on your journey, but I've got a good feeling about you. You have a certain presence, you know? Just promise me something." Kyro turned and looked over at me.

"Remember that you are a champion. A winner. Never lose sight of that. Whether you are at the lowest of lows, or you're on the top of the world. That should never change who you are inside."

I told Kyro that I understood and we proceeded to exit the parking garage.

"Thank you so much for getting me out of the garage and for the ticket to your seminar, Kyro," I said as I put my hand on the latch to open the door.

Kyro looked at my backpack then looked at me. "What's your purpose, Ryko? What are you looking for on your journey?"

"Well, like you talked about tonight, I do know my purpose already. I've felt it my whole life. It's to make a real difference in cats' lives. To touch the lives of many around the world. To do good. To inspire good. And, well, I don't know how, really, or what's in store for me, but I trust the process," I said.

Kyro lifted his paw for a high five and I reached over and slapped his paw. "You're on the right track, little buddy. Enjoy your journey. And hey, if you ever need anything, here's my private business card."

I accepted Kyro's business card as I opened the door and got out of the car. "Thanks again, Kyro. Good night!"

Kyro winked and took off the moment the door was closed. The sound of the Catley echoed off the surrounding buildings and I was sure that every cat in Las Vegas could feel the ground shake as it drove down the road.

I unzipped my backpack, opened my journal, and taped Kyro's

business card on the page of addresses I collected since starting my journey.

It was late. I was tired. And thankfully, I had over 151,287 hotel rooms to choose from.

Vegas, baby.

As I walked to the hotel, I pulled out my notebook and wrote down a few notes:

Be a champion, but not cocky. Be grateful, but reserved. Don't wear headbands with a suit. Somehow decipher the fourteen pages of notes I took from Kyro's seminar. Own a Catley.

ENTRY 15

CAT-NABBIT! I had done it again.

As the train began to leave the station, I realized I had forgotten to mail a postcard to my parents. I was bummed. Las Vegas was a really interesting place, but honestly, I would have no idea how to share my experiences with Kyro using just the backside of a postcard.

One of the train workers walked by, and I asked what the next stop was. I was told Redondo Beach, California. That not only sounded like the perfect place to mail a postcard from, but hanging out on a beach sounded amazing.

I looked out the window and watched the scenery pass by. Thoughts of things Kyro said and his amazing Catley danced around my head. I then realized that I hadn't spent any time cat-napping since I started my journey. I decided not to beat myself up over it and to just enjoy the journey.

We arrived at the Redondo Beach train station, and I followed the signs to the beach. I sat on the largest beach I had ever seen and watched cats surf giant waves in the distance. It was peaceful, but at the same time, I felt an urge to get up and go. Yes, to get a postcard and pee. Seeing so much sand just does the trick for me, I guess.

I walked over to a small shop and looked around the postcards. I found an amazing one that said "Redondo Beach" in big letters on the top. And then it said "Surf's Up!" under it. It had a picture of a cat surfing and giving a paw's up. Perfect.

I purchased the postcard, wrote to my mother and father, got a stamp, and put it into the mail.

As I walked around the beach, something didn't feel quite right. At first I thought it was the fried dough I ate earlier (thank goodness for all the sand), but this feeling was different.

I sat down and tried to figure out the source of this strange feeling. So far this journey has been amazing. I've met some great new friends and I've seen some amazing places, I thought to myself.

And then it hit me. I've mainly just been enjoying the ride and going to the places where everyone goes. I feel like I'm not meant to be like everyone. I more than feel that. I know it.

I often wondered what it would feel like to know when it's time. Time to break free from the paths everyone else takes. Break free from everything and everyone and really get down to some serious business.

To figure out what this thing is inside of me that keeps calling me to do something… And what that something is.

I needed to get out of there.

After walking for several hours, my paws were aching. So I decided to paw some rides out of town. I soon realized that the further away I got from the busy cities, the better I started to feel.

From one paw ride to the next, I bounced from town to town for the next couple of weeks. I did hang my hat in Edmonds, Washington for a few days to take a break from traveling and to mail my parents a postcard.

Unfortunately, the choices for postcards were slim. In fact, there was only one. It said "Edmonds, Washington" on the top and had a black and white photo of the town. I tried to make the postcard a little more exciting by drawing a picture of myself standing on the sidewalk, holding a fish.

Since I was so close to a place I had always dreamed of visiting since I was a little cat, Anchorage, Alaska, I decided to take a train there. It was great, wonderful, beautiful, and the scenery on the train ride was majestic.

The best part of that trip though was the postcard I got my parents. It said "Anchorage, Alaska" on the top of it in big letters, and it had a picture of a bear on the front. I drew myself sitting on the bear's shoulder and wrote how I made a new friend. I'm sure my parents got a kick out of that one.

But it was on the train back down to Washington that was a bit of a defining moment for me on my journey.

For one, it was nighttime, and I wasn't distracted by the scenery outside my window. I had nothing but time on my hands, so I allowed my mind to wonder.

Feelings of missing my mother and father hit me hard. Very hard. I did have a good cry and felt that little tug to go back home, especially because I was so far away.

I started to think about the conversation I'd have with my parents when I returned home. They will want to know all about my journey. Sure, I have many great stories to share, but I have yet to uncover anything about my true purpose.

Suddenly, I had this overwhelming feeling that I was just wasting time. It was like my eyes just opened after being asleep and I realized I was completely in the wrong place. I didn't know where I was supposed to be, but I knew it wasn't anywhere near where I was.

This feeling was a little different than the one by the beach. This one had more urgency to it. Sort of like the feeling you get when you really need to use the litter box.

I took out my journal and wrote:

I'm tired of my journey on the surface. I'm ready to go deeper. To find my purpose. My calling. What I'm supposed to do. How can I make a real difference in this world? Where do I need to go to find this? Or who do I have to become for it to find me?

I took out a map and started to make a plan for a new type of journey.

A journey to find myself.

ENTRY 16

I COULDN'T BELIEVE how much fun I was having at the festival. Who would have thought that I would actually be dancing and enjoying it?

Although I have less dance moves than a caterpillar, I surprised myself out there. I can say that I have officially shaken what my mother has given me and I discovered a new love for live music, especially the band Nine Foot Whiskers.

I'll admit, when their name was announced before they took the stage, I didn't know what to expect. Did they really have whiskers that were nine feet long? How do they manage to walk around?

Thankfully, when they took the stage, their whiskers were normal length. I enjoyed their music so much I ended up getting one of their t-shirts that had a large NFW on the front, and a small Nine Foot Whiskers under it.

I also discovered something interesting. I could actually see and feel the passion coming from many of the singers. These cool cats found their calling and purpose and were owning it. Unlike a lot of other professions, we got to see someone actually living and breathing it, right in front of us. Seeing that inspired me. Their energy inspired me.

Memphis, Tennessee had my toes tapping for days. Besides the music festival, I bounced around from one live music venue to the next. And the most surprising thing of all, I actually wrote this in my journal:

Goal: Start a band someday.

No, as much as it probably disappoints you as it does me, becoming a famous band member is not my calling, but I think it would be so much fun. However, I do have a few skills running across a piano.

I also got a chance to tour Catland, which is the famous former home of the legend, Catvis Meowly.

But there wasn't enough rump-shaking or touristy things I could have done in a thousand years to compare to what happened to me one day in Memphis. It will honestly be a day that I will remember for the rest of my life.

I had planned to spend my last day in Memphis just hanging out and listening to music before I set off on foot to continue the journey I had mapped out.

The morning began by taking a bath by the pool, followed by a wonderful breakfast on the patio overlooking a nearby park.

When I finished eating, I decided to go for a walk in the park because it was such a beautiful morning. I strolled through the park and saw a stage being set up. I walked over to the sign and it said that there was a band playing at 11 AM. Perfect.

With some time to kill, I walked to town and stopped off at a gift shop to pick up a postcard to mail to my mother and father. I found one that said, "Memphis' ' on the top in big letters with a picture of a band playing and people dancing around under it.

I, of course, drew a picture of me dancing and wrote that I was having fun shaking what my mother gave me. I didn't know for sure if they would understand that. I just hoped my mother didn't think that I was shaking the snacks and apple cake she gave me.

Unfortunately, those snacks and cake were long gone.

I sure would've liked a piece of warm apple cake right then. Yum.

I mailed the postcard and walked back to the park.

It was 10:45 in the morning, and there was quite a crowd gathering already. I missed my shot at getting a seat close to the stage, so I decided to go way back by the trees and lay down in the shade.

As I laid down, I kept my backpack on since I learned my lesson the hard way in Denver. I watched as other cats made their way to the stage area to find a place to sit.

Then something caught my eye. I slowly sat up as my jaw hit the ground.

Suddenly, everything became blurry all around me except for the one thing I was starting to see appear through the crowd.

I slowly stood up and my heart began to race.

What I saw and felt at that very moment... I'm really struggling to find the words. I just sat here for over an hour zoning out recalling that exact moment in time. I'm going to try my best to explain the unexplainable.

It was almost as if time itself slowed down. Everything around me moved in slow motion. My senses were heightened to levels I had never experienced.

I could hear conversations a hundred yards away with ease, yet their words didn't distract me.

I could smell the pizza being made over a mile away, but the smell of cheese didn't deter me.

I could feel literally every single hair on my body stand up ever so slightly.

I could taste the air, which was lightly sweetened by the flowers over a half a mile away.

And I could see *her*.

As I looked at her, she slowly turned my way, and began walking towards me.

It was if the crowd parted, and all that existed was her and I in that space and time.

She was the most beautiful cat I had ever seen. Every step she took towards me melted my heart more and more until I was just one pile of mush.

Her nose, her ears, her eyes, her everything was absolutely and truly perfect.

I was afraid to blink because I didn't want to lose one millisecond of looking at her.

I clearly remember thinking to myself, "So this is what love feels like. This is what my parents have." And I remember saying to myself, "I want to feel this each and every single day for the rest of my life with this beautiful cat jogging towards me."

Wait. She's jogging towards... me?

She continued to get closer and closer. She smiled, and I nearly fell over from the feeling of warmth, kindness, and gentleness she had.

And then she waved as she ran towards me faster with her arms wide open.

I then extended my arms and closed my eyes just as we were about to meet and hug. And then... I continued to stand there. And I stood there. Yup. Still standing there with my arms wide open.

Alone.

I opened my eyes as I heard the most beautiful southern accent voice I have ever heard say, "Hey, how are you?" I looked over to my right and my melted heart just simply faded away as I saw the most beautiful cat I have ever laid my eyes on hugging some guy cat next to me.

My eyes fell to the ground, followed by my body. I just sat there. Devastated. Deflated. My heart was filled with such overwhelming and overpowering love for the first time in my life, only to have it stripped away. All within seconds. How is that even possible?

The band played song after song. I didn't move a muscle. I just looked at the ground in a daze.

After the concert ended and nearly everyone left, I looked up for the first time. I just didn't understand. What in the world just happened to me? How was that whole experience even possible?

I honestly didn't know what to think. This certainly was not an experience anyone had ever told me about. I mean, am I crazy? Is it even possible to see someone, just see them, not even talk to them, and fall head over heels in love with them?

I was taught that whenever I have a bad experience that I need to try and find the good in it and be grateful for the experience. Always easier said than done. And in this case, absolutely and completely impossible.

I stood up from the ground as a different cat that evening. One with a scar that would forever be imprinted on my heart, even though I wasn't exactly sure why.

As I lay in bed that evening, I had my journal open in front of me. I just looked at the page, trying to find words to describe what had transpired. There was nothing I could come up with that could truly explain the journey of the highest of highs to the lowest of lows in a matter of seconds. So I just wrote:

Memphis. Ouch.

ENTRY 17

I BARELY SLEPT.

I just kept reliving those few seconds when I saw her walking and running towards me. I felt like an idiot because I thought she was feeling what I was feeling and was running up to hug me.

My pain slowly turned into anger at myself and then anger at the situation, then back to anger at myself for choosing to sit at that park. I thought, "If I just would have picked a different place this crazy situation wouldn't have happened and I wouldn't be feeling this way".

I didn't ask for this. Not even in the slightest bit.

It was nearly 11:00 AM when I got out of bed, which was much later than usual. After my bath, I just sat there thinking. Then I realized that the wind was gone. The wind had never been gone before.

For as long as I can remember, there's always been wind blowing my sail, always pushing me forward. It was in many ways, my guide to help steer me in the right direction. But for the first time that I was aware of, the wind was gone.

I stood up and literally said out loud, "Oh great. This girl, who I don't even know, not only stole my heart, but she stole my wind. I am never, and I mean never, sitting under a tree again. I somehow got everything stolen from me, even when it's inside of me!"

I looked over at my backpack on the chair and my map on the table. Leaving today was not going to happen. I didn't feel like it. I wasn't even excited about it. I just wasn't myself.

Despite everything going on, I was getting really hungry. The only thing that I could decide was that having ice cream for breakfast was a good idea.

As I walked out of the room, I somehow got my foot tangled in the cord to the iron, and I took a nosedive right into the wall. I got up, patted my nose, and saw there was some blood. I got up, grabbed a towel, and sat on the bed, holding my nose.

I just shook my head at the iron. Mostly, I shook my head at whomever invented the self-wrapping cord that's connected to irons. Why? Because out of all the hotel rooms I've ever stayed in, I can count one, maybe two, that actually worked properly.

Once the bleeding stopped, I walked out of my room and pressed the button on the elevator to go down. A few minutes passed by, and I pressed it again. And again. Nothing.

I sighed and walked to the stairs and proceeded to go down ten flights of stairs.

Once outside, I walked to an ice cream shop and sat down at one of the tables outside. As I was looking at the menu, I nearly had a heart attack when I heard, "Hi sweetie, what can I get for you?"

I slowly looked up to confirm what my ears had just heard and yes, *IT WAS HER.*

I became frozen and could not even speak. I just looked at her.

"You alright honey?" she asked.

I mustered up every single ounce of cat power I had inside my body, snapped out of it, and said, "Oh yes. I'm fine. I'll have a love shake... Chocolate! I'll have a chocolate shake. Um, I love them, I mean, chocolate."

As I stumbled for my words, I looked down at her name tag. It said Kory.

"Chocolate shake, got it. And hey, did you get into a fight? What happened to your nose?" Kory asked.

"Sort of," I replied. "The cord to the iron and the wall unfortunately won."

Kory laughed. Just hearing her laugh somehow resurrected my heart only so it could begin to melt again. But honestly, I did not care one bit. It felt so amazing to be next to her.

"Wait a second. Do I know you?" Kory asked as she put her notepad into a pocket in her apron.

"I don't think so," I said.

"Yeah, yeah," Kory said thinking as she tapped her pen to her lip. "Yesterday at the concert. I felt so bad. I saw you and I wanted to say something, but you looked pretty busy watching ants or something on the ground."

"Oh, well, um, you see, I ummm, I" I stumbled.

"I thought maybe we knew each other from somewhere, maybe school?" Kory said in the cutest southern voice ever, as my heart melted and melted some more into a pile of mush. "And you wanted to give me a hug."

I was frozen again.

"Well, I'm so sorry about that!" Kory said, as she took the menu from the table. "I hadn't seen my brother for a whole year while he went on his journey, and I was just so surprised to see him. I'll be back with your shake!"

Wait. Brother? Not boyfriend? Not husband? Brother?

Think, Ryko, think. Snap out of this strange love trance. It's time to put on the Ryko charm.

I thought about all the amazing things I could say to Kory when she came back. I had at least ten amazing things and at least another ten back ups, depending how the conversation went.

After a few minutes, Kory came back with my chocolate shake, and sat it down on the table.

I looked up at her, and, well, my mind went totally blank. The only two words I could string together were, "Thank you."

Kory smiled, said, "You're welcome, sweetie," and walked away to take the order of a couple that had just sat down across from me.

My paws were sweaty. My heart was beating a thousand miles an hour. How on earth could this be? Who is this Kory cat? Why does she have such a profound effect on me? And how do I shut it off? Most importantly, do I even want to shut it off?

As I was having a rather confusing and complicated discussion in my head, Kory walked by my table. "Everything tasting good over here?" she said with a smile bright enough to melt a million hearts from a thousand miles away.

"Can I take you out for milk when you get off work?" I somehow said. I promise, this was not one of the twenty amazing things I had planned on saying. Honestly and truthfully, I have no idea where that came from.

Kory kneeled down by my table, took a few more chews of her gum, and said, "Well, it depends."

"On?" I replied.

"Two things. One, you tell me your name, and two, if we make it chocolate milk."

I smiled, nodded, and said, "Done and done. I mean Ryko and done. I mean...."

Kory giggled, "OK, Ryko Done. Swing back by here at 3:00. I know of a great chocolate milk place up the road. See you then sweetie!"

I took a sip of my melting chocolate shake.

I let out a little smile as I thought to myself, "And this is where my real journey begins."

ENTRY 18

I ARRIVED AT THE ICE CREAM SHOP at 2:55, just as Kory was walking down the stairs.

"Perfect timing, Ryko Done. A cat on time, that's always a good sign, at least that's what my momma tells me," Kory said, as she ran her paw through her hair.

I laughed, "Well, my name isn't exactly Ryko Done. It's just Ryko."

"I know, just go with it," Kory said.

As we walked to the chocolate milk shop, I was finally finding my footing around Kory. And by the time we arrived, I was able to actually gather my thoughts and have a normal conversation.

But I will admit, every time she ran her paw through her hair, it would make the hair on the back of my neck start to stand up. I hope she didn't notice.

We got to the chocolate milk shop, and I quickly got in front of Kory to open the door for her.

"My goodness," Kory said with a smile. "You were obviously not raised in a barn. I'm impressed by your manners!"

"Well, thank you, Kory! I do have excellent parents who taught me how to treat a lady," I said as Kory walked into the restaurant.

"Table for two?" the waiter cat asked. "Yes," I said, as I extended my paw out for Kory to walk in front of me.

We sat down at a table that overlooked a fountain in the court-yard outside.

"I'm telling you, Ryko," Kory said as she put her purse down beside her chair, "you've never had chocolate milk until you've had chocolate milk from here. It's delicious."

"Well, I'm looking forward to it, Kory. So, I take it you are from Memphis?"

"Oh no, that's a long story. I'm from a lot of places. I'm just here for awhile, to work and save up some money. Enough about me, I'm wondering about where you're from. Your backpack is a dead giveaway that you're on your journey, you know."

I looked down at my back park and laughed. "You got me. It is a dead giveaway, isn't it? Well, I'm from New Hampshire, and have been on my journey for awhile. Been to many places, done many things, but just getting started in a lot of ways."

"Oh, I know exactly what you mean, I actually..." Kory started to say before she was interrupted by the waiter.

"Hi. I'm Morrie. What can I get for you this evening? Wait, would you like to know about our specials?" the waiter asked.

Kory passed on the specials and asked the waiter for a double chocolate milk with a little whip cream and two cherries.

The waiter wrote down her order and looked at me. I replied, "The same please."

The waiter closed his book. "Great, I'll be back with your double chocolate milks shortly!"

"As I was saying, about the journey, I..."

"I'm so sorry," the waiter interrupted. "Sir, did you want one or two cherries with your chocolate milk?"

"Two is fine," I replied. And the waiter ran off.

Kory smiled about the interruptions. Our eyes locked. Her eyes were like a magnet. I not only could not take my eyes off of her, but her eyes drew me in unlike anything I had ever experienced before. Looking at Kory gave me a feeling that I cannot adequately describe with words.

Usually when you are talking to someone, anyone really, you start to feel that funny feeling when you're looking into their eyes for too long, so you look away for a moment. Not with Kory. I could easily look into her eyes forever and never ever look away.

A good six or seven seconds passed as we looked into each others' eyes. Kory looked away, shook her head slightly, and said, "Sorry, what were we talking about?"

"You were saying something about the journey," I responded.

"Oh yes, so a funny, random fact about me is that I…"

"And here are your chocolate milks!" The waiter placed both chocolate milks on the table. I immediately noticed that neither had any cherries on them. I could tell Kory had noticed that and was probably annoyed at getting interrupted so many times.

"Thank you, sir," Kory said in a kind, southern voice. "Can we please have two to go cups, as well as a cup of cherries?"

"Sure, I'll be right back." The waiter turned around.

"Hold on," I said, catching on to what Kory was up to. "Here's the money for the chocolate milks."

"How about I continue what I was trying to say on the bench by the fountain outside?" Kory suggested.

"I was thinking the same exact thing," I said, laughing.

The waiter delivered three to go cups, two with cherries and one empty cup. Kory laughed and dumped half of the cherries in her chocolate milk, the other half in mine, and we poured our chocolate milks into the to-go cups. We left the other cup of cherries on the table.

"Rookies," Kory said with a smirk.

Kory and I walked outside and found a bench by the fountain, free of distractions. In fact, we were the only cats out there. We had the place to ourselves.

"What do you think of the chocolate milk? Not the service, but the milk?" Kory said laughing.

I took a sip and it was as if I had just tasted heaven. "Are you kidding me!?" I said, right before taking another sip. "This is truly the best chocolate milk ever. Excellent choice!"

"Glad you like it," Kory said, right before she ate a cherry. "So as I was trying to say," Kory said laughing, "Would you believe that I have been on the journey four different times?"

"Four?" I said with a mouth full of chocolate milk. A little dribbled on my chin, which I quickly wiped away with my paw.

"I know, I know. You're probably thinking, 'Oh no, here's a hot mess of a girl who has no idea what she wants,' right? But that's not at all the case. I have always known, and I absolutely love going on the journey. Just getting up and going, without a plan, or direction, or a clue. I love it!" Kory said, as she took a sip of her chocolate milk.

"So hold on a second," I said, as I raised my paw for added effect. "There are two big things here. One, you have always known, and two, you just love going on journeys?"

Kory popped another cherry in her mouth and said, "That's right! Ever since I was a little kitten, I knew I wanted to be a fashion designer. It's so fun. Cats say I'm a natural and I never feel like I'm working when I m designing. So I didn't go on my journeys to discover myself, I went on them to discover more about myself and because I just love to get up and go somewhere on a whim. For example, during my last journey, I learned that I also love making jewelry."

I slurped the last few drops of my chocolate milk. "You know Kory, I must say, I'm impressed. For one, you know exactly what your calling is, and two, you just love to go on journeys so much. That's something I have not heard before."

Kory smiled. "My momma says I'm as spontaneous as they come. And that's saying a lot because she's raised thirty-two cats."

"You have thirty-one brothers and sisters? How is that even possible?" I asked.

"Well, I really don't know if I have any real brothers or sisters. And honestly, I never really admit this to anyone, but I'm adopted. My momma adopted me a couple years ago, shortly after I had gone on my first journey and ended up in Memphis. Before that, I had four other foster cat parents, so I moved around a lot." Kory said.

"Oh wow. So you're used to bouncing around. I can see why you like to go on journeys all the time. I think that is great!" I said.

Kory ran her paw through her hair. "Kittenhood was a tough time. Very tough. I wouldn't wish what I've been through on any cat..."

Kory looked down at the ground as she spoke. I could tell that as she spoke those words there was a lot of pain buried deep. In fact, I could more than just tell; I could feel it. I quickly changed the subject.

"Are you doing your fashion designing here in Memphis?" I asked.

Kory finished her chocolate milk and bit into the last cherry she had in her cup. "I don't know where I'll end up designing clothing or jewelry. Maybe L.A., New York, Chicago, I don't know. I just have two months of school left and then I can figure that out."

"That's great, congratulations!" I said with a smile, "Well, an early congratulations, about school."

Kory giggled, "Well, thank you. I actually go back to Austin tomorrow to finish school. From there, who knows, which is really exciting to me."

"No way! I was just in Austin a little while ago. You have to go standing surfboard riding. It's a blast!" I said.

"You mean paddleboarding?" Kory laughed. "Oh yes, I've done it many times. So what were you doing in Austin?"

"Just hopped off the train, and there I was." I said. "I hung out there, met some cool cats, and continued to Denver, Las Vegas, and some places on the west coast, and even Alaska."

Kory adjusted so her body was facing me. "Wait a second. Train? Let me guess, you have a map in your backpack, don't you?"

I looked down at my backpack. "Um, yes."

"No, no, silly. Forget taking the train, use those four paws of yours and follow your heart. It's how they did it back in the old days. It's the real way to take the journey, the authentic journey, as I like to call it." Kory said.

I reached into my backpack, grabbed my map, and pulled it out. "It's funny you say that. I had a weird feeling in California and again when I was leaving Alaska that something wasn't quite right. Starting here, I decided to go about my journey on foot and planned out a long winding path to make it back to New Hampshire before winter."

I opened up the map, and Kory slid right next to me so she could see it.

It was at this very moment that I wished I had a button so I could pause time forever. The temptation to give her a hug was nearly impossible to resist. And her perfume. It was driving me crazy. Breathe, Ryko. Calm yourself. Breathe. Cat ball. Breathe.

"Ryko, Ryko, Ryko. I'm going to do something that you are either going to love me or hate me forever for."

I had a lot to say to that statement, but before I could open my mouth, Kory stood up, took the map out of my hands, and ripped it up into dozens of pieces and threw it into the trash that was next to the bench across from us.

"Now, my friend, your journey to finding Ryko officially begins. No maps. No directions. No worries. Just open woods, open fields, and an open mind. That's the only way to travel, I say," Kory said with a giant smirk on her face, and she wiped her paws.

Funny thing was, watching her rip up my map gave me some relief. I actually did feel a sense of freedom wash over me when she tossed it into the trash.

"Kory, I only have one thing to say," I said as I pretended to get mad, "regarding your comment before you tore up my map... I'm probably going to end up loving you forever." We both laughed for a while and then our eyes locked in on each other.

This time it was even more intense than it was at the restaurant. We were closer to each other and I could easily make out the fine details of her eyes. They drew me in even deeper and I felt myself slowly moving towards them.

Kory blinked her eyes quickly, looked away, and shook her head a few times to snap out of it. It was at that very moment that I could tell she felt something, too. I have no idea if it was even in the same universe as the feelings I felt, but I knew she felt something. I'm sure of it. Positive. I mean, I hope she did.

Kory looked over at me and asked, "So have you figured it out, Ryko?"

I wasn't quite sure if Kory was referring to us, our eyes locking, or what with this question. She could see I was perplexed.

"Do you know what your calling is?" Kory asked.

"Oh, well, yes and no. It's actually really complicated. But long story short, ever since I was a little kitten, I have always felt I was meant for something big. To make a big difference. To somehow have a positive impact on the lives of countless cats around the world. My parents always told me that, too. But I don't know what, how, or any details yet. I just know that feeling has always lived inside of me."

As Kory absorbed what I had said, I continued. "One thing I do know, is that a big part of helping other cats is through adoption and rescues. I know that's going to play a large role in what I do. I don't know if it's the main role or a piece of it. But I know I'm going to figure it out."

As I said this to Kory, she had looked away from me and out towards the trees in the distance. As I was talking, I didn't know if something caught her eye in the park or if it was nothing.

Kory slowly moved her left paw up by her eyes, slowly wiped them, and as she put her paw down, I could see her fur was wet.

"Oh my God, I'm so sorry, did I say something to upset you?" I asked Kory.

"No, no. You didn't," Kory said softly.

We sat in silence for over a minute. I didn't know if I should talk, give her a hug, or what to do. I was frozen and I felt really bad.

"Look," Kory said as she wiped her eyes again. "I'm going to tell you something that I never ever talk about. You hit a pretty big nerve with me, but please don't feel bad. You didn't know."

I reached into my backpack and took out a few napkins and handed them to Kory.

"Thank you," she said as she wiped her eyes. She looked off into the distance, and another moment passed.

"I'm a rescue, Ryko," Kory said as she started to cry.

I put my arm around her, and she put her head on my chest.

As she cried, my eyes welled up with tears, and one slowly rolled off my cheek and landed on her ear. Her ear twitched and she slowly looked up at me.

"Wait. What? You're crying too?" Kory asked.

"OK you caught me," I said with a smile, trying to lighten the mood. "What can I say, I'm not like most guy cats. I'm an emotional cat. You shared something with me that you don't talk about and now I shared something that I actually try to hide."

We both laughed a little.

Kory put her head back down on my chest and I slowly put my arm around her.

There are zero words to describe what I was feeling at that moment. I would have done anything, literally anything in the world to make the pain Kory was feeling just go away.

"I've never shared the details with anyone," Kory said. "I don't think I ever could because I just couldn't relive what I went through again. But I do thank God each and every single day that I was rescued when I was a kitten. I know I wouldn't be here today if I wasn't."

"Kory, I am so sorry," I said.

Kory lifted her head up from my chest. She started to laugh a little. "I'm so sorry. I promise I'm not an emotional mess. I haven't cried in a few years, probably. But you got me when you mentioned that you want to help somehow with cat adoptions and rescues. The reason why I'm getting into fashion and jewelry is because my ultimate dream, my goal, and my purpose, is to run cat adoption centers all around the world and save millions of cats."

As Kory said this, the hair around my neck stood straight up. I was a giant puffball. Normally I'd get embarrassed, but for some reason, I didn't around Kory.

She reached her paw around me and tried to push my hair back down, but it kept popping back up. She started giggling, and I giggled too.

I had never felt the feelings Kory stirred up inside of me. I literally just wanted to stay on the bench with her and talk for the rest of my life. I wished time would slow down because it was starting to get dark and there were no lights where we were by the fountain.

We sat together for several more minutes... Minutes I will forever cherish.

"It's getting dark. Can I have the honor of walking you home, Kory?"

"Being the fine New Hampshire gentleman you are, Ryko, I would not expect anything less," Kory said as she playfully jabbed my side.

As we walked to Kory's house, I felt like I was walking on air. I had never felt so light. And that's saying a lot considering all of the cake and ice cream I have been eating lately. Ugh. I should start thinking about doing the Cato Diet once I get back to New Hampshire, I thought to myself.

"So tomorrow, I'm off to Austin to finish school and you are off to who knows where on your journey. These are exciting times for both of us," Kory said as we walked slowly to extend the time we had together.

"Yes, thanks to you I now have no idea where I am going. And I admit, I am pretty excited about that!" I said, laughing.

"Well, this is my momma's house. It's where I live, well, right now anyway," Kory said softly.

"Look, I'm the type of cat who can write words much better than I can speak them, let me do my best here." I took Kory's paws and stood in front of her. "Kory, I think you are the most amazing cat I have ever met in my life. You make me feel all sorts of crazy inside. If my entire journey, if my entire life's purpose all led to today, to spend time with you, I will be forever grateful. But I do hope there will be more. A lot more. Like, a lot, a lot more. Like a lot a..."

Kory giggled. "I know what you mean Ryko. Let me know when you get home. I want to hear about your journey and where this new path takes you."

I reached into my backpack and took out my journal. "Would you mind writing down your address so I can mail you a letter when I get back home?" I asked.

Kory took my journal and pen, wrote for a while, and then closed my journal.

"Thank you, Ryko. I had a great time."

"Thank you, Kory. I did as well."

I slowly backed up ten steps from Kory and looked at her for a moment. I closed my eyes and slowly opened my arms.

I heard running in front of me and felt a giant hug. I closed my arms around Kory. We hugged for several seconds and I heard a slight purr. Kory slowly let go.

"Enjoy your journey, Ryko," Kory said, as she walked down the walkway towards her house.

"Have fun at school and I'll be in touch soon," I said.

Kory walked up to the door. She opened it, walked inside, and turned around. She waved as I waved back and then she closed the door.

I stood there for a moment, just soaking it all in.

Wow. I was in awe of so many things and wasn't sure which one to think about first.

I walked back to my hotel and it still felt as if I was walking on air.

When I walked into my room, I noticed that there was a new iron sitting on the counter. One that actually had the cord wrapped inside of it. Nice.

I also saw a handwritten note laying on the bed. It read:

Please do not use white towels for blood. You have been charged a $3 service fee for a new towel. Thank you, Hotel Staff

The letter didn't phase me. At this point, nothing in the world could phase me. I was happy.

I got into bed and took out my journal. I flipped to the page Kory wrote on. She said:

Follow your heart, not the rails or trails. It's the only map you will ever need. - xoxo Kory

And then she shared her address. Which by the way, I am not going to share in this book or anywhere for obvious reasons. I need to minimize my competition, you know.

Thinking back to Kory ripping up my map that had my route all planned out and reading what she wrote really hit a nerve in me. Not at all in a bad way, of course. It felt like I'd been holding onto a rope this whole time and now that rope was severed.

She was right. Thinking back to the hundreds of times I went off into the woods in New Hampshire to explore and catnap, some of the most profound experiences I had were when I was off the beaten path. Although scratching my own path through the forest wasn't easy at times, I almost always found something that made my little adventures worth it.

I reached over to the nightstand, grabbed a pen, and started writing down my experiences and thoughts about the incredible day I just had.

Now for several reasons, I'm only going to reprint a few things that I wrote. Truth be told, I wrote thirteen pages in my journal about Kory that night. Much of it was very personal, and I would be embarrassed to put it all in this book. But here's a few things that I can share with you:

Everyone has the power to leave an everlasting, loving footprint on your heart. As do you. Use that power wisely.

Sometimes it takes going into the darkness in order to prepare you to see the light.

Imagine if every rescued cat was as amazing as Kory. How many would you want to rescue?

Try to get the recipe for the chocolate milk I had with Kory tonight. At all costs.

If that was love, it is the absolute craziest emotion a cat can feel. It can make you happy, sad, crazy, calm, content, uneasy, scared, confident, and confused all at the exact same time. Wow.

Our hearts are the best map.

ENTRY 19

WHEN I OPENED MY EYES, the sun was just starting to rise. I got out of my bed and walked over to the window to watch the beauty that is the sunrise.

I thought about how I did the same thing when I first left home for my journey. I thought about my parents watching me and giving me a huge hug. Oh, I missed them dearly, but I fought back the tears and allowed a big smile to take over my face.

"Everything in my journey has led me to this day," I thought to myself. "Today is when my real journey begins. It's time to finally realize my purpose, my mission, and the source of the tug on my heart."

I packed my things, went downstairs, and enjoyed a large bowl of oatmeal and berries for breakfast. When I finished, I walked outside and stood on the sidewalk. I looked left, then right, and closed my eyes.

I imagined myself walking left and felt how that would feel.

Then I imagined walking right and felt that feeling. Right it is. And so I went.

It wasn't too long that I was away from the hustle and bustle of Memphis when I saw a sign for the Meeman-Shelby Forest State Park. I decided to follow the signs to the park and soon came upon a river.

I leaned down and took a few sips of water. I looked upstream, then downstream, and thought for a moment. I chose to follow the river upstream.

Going the path less traveled (or in this case, maybe never) wasn't easy. I had to claw my way through several parts where the brush was really thick. It was slow going at times. Making your own path is obviously a lot of hard work, but I was really enjoying myself and the feeling of freedom.

After many hours, I felt it was time to leave the riverbanks. I leaned down to take another sip of water, stood back up, tightened my backpack, and closed my eyes.

This time I imagined a giant compass in front of me with the needle going round and round. I watched the red tip of the needle eventually slow down and come to a stop. It pointed to my right and off I went.

For more days than I can recall, I made my way through the forest, fields, and even through a few small towns. As I continued to walk, I started to see some mountains appear in the distance. I felt that was the direction I needed to go.

I walked up and down many hills, and as I walked, the forest became more and more dense. Trees and leaves were all I could see. Soon, I wasn't able to see which direction the mountains were, so I truly had no idea if I was going the right direction or not.

There has to be a way to see the mountains, I thought. I stopped for a moment and looked around. I spotted a large, tall tree that had many branches. It looked like a very simple climb, so I walked over to it and began making my way up.

The tree was nearly made for climbing. Strong, thick branches were spaced apart in a way that made it like climbing a spiral staircase. As I made my way up higher and higher in the tree, I noticed that it became brighter, so I knew I was near a clearing where I could see which direction the mountains were.

As I was looking around me, I wasn't paying close attention to where I was putting my paws. I reached up with my left paw and it felt like my paw went right into a thick paper bag filled with glue.

I froze, looked down, and I felt a wave of pure terror wash over me after seeing what I had just done.

Within seconds, a cloud of bees surrounded me. I quickly pulled my paw out of the beehive and frantically began to make my way back down the tree.

I felt a bee sting my right leg. I meowed. I made my way down the tree faster.

Then I was stung on my right paw. I nearly slipped off a branch as I let out a loud, "Ouch!"

And then it felt like I jumped into a pile of needles as I felt several stings all at once on my face, ears, back, stomach, tail, and all four legs.

I let out a screeching meow from the pain.

I saw that I was still very high in the tree, so jumping was not an option. My heart was pounding a thousand beats per second. I was terrified. The pain was unbearable.

"No, no, no!" I screamed. "This cannot be happening!" For the first time in my life, I wondered if I was about to die.

I felt another half a dozen stings on my back and side.

No. Please. No.

For a few seconds, I continued to climb down but very quickly noticed that my body was going completely numb. My legs, arms, and paws weren't going where I wanted to go. I couldn't see out of my right eye. I reached for a branch and missed.

And down the tree I went, tumbling over and over, off every branch as I fell to the ground. I hit the ground hard.

Everything went black.

ENTRY 20

It was the most amazing thing I had ever seen.

It was completely black all around me, except a large blue, white, and purple ball that seemed to float there. It was full of energy. All the colors danced around inside and outside of it quickly, like millions of tiny lightning bolts. I had no idea what I was looking at. I had never seen anything like it before.

Suddenly I heard, "Ryko…. Ryko…. Ryko…" off in the very far distance.

I felt as if I was moving, looked down, and saw nothing but darkness. Suddenly, I felt as if I was moving a thousand miles an hour.

"Ryko," it sounded like someone was saying my name, right into my ears.

Slowly, I began to feel the presence of something against my back. As seconds passed, I started to feel my body and could tell that I was laying down.

"Ryko," the voice said again. I opened my mouth to speak, but no words came out.

I drifted off.

Time passed. How much, I wouldn't even begin to guess. I felt awake and more present than before, but this time I felt pain. Everywhere there was pain. I let out a soft meow.

"Ryko," the voice said again.

"Hello?" I said softly.

"You're OK. Everything is going to be OK. Just relax," the voice said.

"Where am I?" I asked.

"You're at my house. None of that matters now. Rest. You're OK... You're OK... You're..."

I drifted off back to sleep.

I was startled by a noise, followed by a loud crash that seemed to go on forever. I opened my eyes as I heard, "Oh gosh, I am so sorry! I've been as quiet as a mouse for days and somehow I ended up knocking down every pot and pan I own onto the floor. Ah, your eyes are open! Good!"

As my eyes began to focus, I could see that I was in a cave of sorts. Or maybe inside of a tree? It was hard to tell. What happened? Where am I? What is going on? Who is this person? My mind started to race.

I looked over to my left as I saw a cat approach me.

"I do not know how long you were laying there, but it was good I found you when I did because I don't think you would have made it," the cat said.

As my eyes adjusted, I looked at the cat that was speaking to me. He was an older cat, really rough around the edges. His hair was black and gray, striped in places. He had a very thick tail that was quite knotted and had pieces of grass, sticks, and who knows what else stuck to it.

"Who are you? Where am I? And what in the heck is that horrible smell?" I asked.

The smell hit me like a ton of bricks. I had never smelled something so strong, so terrible. It was if my nose hairs were being burned with every breath. I coughed.

"Oh, don't mind that smell," the cat said. "It's what saved your life. It's my own special formula of honey, baking soda, apple cider vinegar, toothpaste, tea tree oil, witch hazel, lavender, olive oil, and goat spit. It heals bee stings in no time."

I looked down at myself and my entire body was practically in a cast of this horrible medley of ingredients.

"Who are you?" I asked.

"Name is Tiger. I'm a Maine Coon, if you haven't figured that out already by my fur and tail."

I carefully licked my nose and accidentally got a taste of the paste that covered my body. After gagging for a moment, I asked Tiger how he knew my name.

"It's on the backpack you had with you. I'm guessing that is your backpack, right?"

"Yeah," I said. "It is."

"I've never seen anyone with so many bee stings. And they must have also hit you a few times with a club or something because you had some nasty bruises all over you," Tiger said as he walked over to a small stand to turn on a light.

I told Tiger about how I was climbing a tree to get my bearings, about the bees, and about falling from the tree.

Tiger walked into his small kitchen, poured something that was steaming into a bowl, and walked over.

"Here, drink this. It doesn't taste good, but it'll help you get back on your feet in no time," Tiger said as he handed me a bowl.

"This smells even worse than what you covered my body with!" I said as I gagged again.

Tiger chuckled. "Just drink it. Please trust me. I've lived in the forest my entire life and know a thing or two about natural remedies."

"I'm not even going to ask what's in here," I said as I drank what tasted like a mixture of swamp water with moldy cheese chunks, dirt, and possibly a worm or two.

"Rest now," Tiger said as he tucked in a blanket around me. You'll be back to yourself in a few days when you wake up."

"Wait, a few days? I can't wait..." I was asleep before I could finish.

ENTRY 21

My eyes popped open and I was wide awake. And truthfully, I felt absolutely amazing.

I looked down and I thankfully did not have any of that horrible paste on me. I was all cleaned up.

I looked around and Tiger wasn't anywhere to be found. I slowly got out of bed, thinking I was going to feel aches and pains all over my body, but I was shocked that I felt absolutely zero pain. In fact, I felt incredible.

I walked over to the kitchen table and saw a letter. It read:

Ryko, I trust you are back to your normal self by now. I have to run to visit my aunt and will be back in a few days.

I assume you will be long gone by then. Take what you need from the fridge.

Watch where you put your paws next time.

Best of luck to you,

Tiger

"Wow," I thought to myself. Even though I had no idea who this cat was, he saved my life and healed me. He did not ask, nor expect anything in return. I was humbled. I flipped the paper over and wrote Tiger a letter expressing my true, heartfelt gratitude the best I could. I mean, what words can you say to someone who saved your life?

I told Tiger that I promised to find a way to thank him someday.

I looked over to the other side of the table and saw a pile of mail. I flipped an envelope over and noticed it had his address on it. I took out my journal and wrote it down.

As I opened the door, the sunlight hit me like a thousand suns. "How long have I been here?" I thought to myself. I truly had no idea. Days? Weeks? Months?

As I closed the door behind me, I looked back and saw that Tiger's house was made from a large tree that had fallen over. He had hollowed out the tree to make several rooms and covered the hole in the ground with sticks and logs that exposed the roots to make a larger room. I was impressed.

And now I was completely, utterly, and officially lost. I had no idea as to what town or even what state I was in. I took a couple deep breaths and allowed the panic of being lost to fade away into nothing.

I closed my eyes and pretended the giant compass was in front of me again. Only this time, the needle kept spinning and spinning. It wouldn't stop. I opened my eyes, shook my head, and just started walking.

Several days passed as I continued walking through this never ending forest. The terrain became quite difficult at times. There were some steep uphills and some very steep downhills where I had to leap from tree to tree to make my way down. This time I made sure that I was extra careful where I put my paws, of course.

As I made my way down a hill, I heard the sound of rushing water get louder and louder. Soon through the trees I could see a small, but rapidly flowing river. By the time I reached the bottom of the hill, the small river ended up being quite wide. The sound of the white water river was the only sound I could hear. I was surprised at how loud it was.

I stood on the riverbank for a moment and tried to come up with a way to cross the river.

"It's moving far too rapidly for me to even think about swimming across," I said to myself.

I decided to work my way upstream along the riverbank to see if the water was any calmer. It wasn't. The water only became rougher and rougher and louder and louder.

After some time, I noticed a tree upstream that had fallen across the raging river. I decided to go check it out.

It looked like the tree had fallen very recently, but I wasn't worried if it was rotten. I climbed on top of it and it was as sturdy as the ground. I looked across the river and the top of the tree was laying on the ground on the other side.

Then I looked at the raging river. It was the roughest river I had ever seen. The water was flowing very quickly, white water was everywhere, and there were giant boulders scattered all throughout the river as far as my eyes could see.

"You got this, Ryko," I said to myself as I took one step forward and then paused.

I thought for a moment about what I was doing. "Why didn't the thought of going the opposite direction, completely avoiding the river even occur to me? Why on earth am I choosing the hardest route anyone could take?" I asked myself.

I didn't know how to answer that besides it just felt right to get to the other side of the river. And so I began.

As I walked down the tree, I noticed that the bark was missing in a large section, nearly halfway down. Fearing it could be slippery, I extended my claws in both my front and back paws.

I could feel the spray of the water on my body and face as I paused for a moment and tested the surface of the tree where the bark was missing with my paw. Just what I feared, it was wet and as slippery as a fish covered in olive oil.

Then I extended my claws on my right paw as far as they could go, dug into the tree, and tested to see if it would hold. It did with no problem at all.

I took a deep breath and extended my left paw, digging it into the tree. I had a firm grip. Perfect.

I proceeded very carefully, one paw in front of the other, thoroughly digging each claw into the tree, ensuring that I had a firm grip with each step.

Suddenly as I was reaching my right paw out, my back left leg lost its grip and slipped off the tree. I panicked and quickly lowered my body to regain my balance.

"Whew," I said. "That was a close one."

Once I had my firm grip back, I continued to take one slow step after another. Several minutes passed and I was just ten or so steps away from where the tree's bark appeared again.

I was gripping tightly with my two front paws as I released the claws in my back left foot. Right then, my right foot lost its grip. Within a second, somehow both of my back legs were hanging off of the side of the tree. I dug my front claws even further into the tree as I tried to get one of my back legs back onto the tree.

For several minutes, I tried to get my left leg back leg up, with no success. Then I tried my right leg. Still, no luck.

I worked very hard to keep my mind focused. I knew that if I started to panic I would put myself in an even worse position. I clung onto the tree with my front paws, trying to come up with another method to get back up onto the tree. My arms were starting to tire.

I decided to start moving my front paws over, carefully, one at a time, to make my way over to where the bark was. I knew once I was at the bark that it would be easy to get my back legs up on the tree and then I would be home free.

I quickly retracted the claws in my left paw and dug them back in a few inches to the left. It worked. I then followed with my right paw. Success.

My arms were burning and tired, but I continued to make my way over towards the bark. One paw at a time.

I reached the bark with my left paw, as I dug in for an extra firm grip. I let out a huge sigh of relief.

I retracted the claws of my right paw, so I could quickly move my paw just a couple of inches over to the left and extend my claws again. It turned out that the shift in my weight while on the bark was too much. To make matters worse, I didn't even realize that the bark was loose, which resulted in it breaking off.

I fell into the water and quickly had zero sense of which way was up, down, or sideways. I tossed and turned as my body bounced from rock to rock underwater.

I held my breath and began to panic. I was flailing my arms, trying to reach for anything I could grab. I managed to grab a rock several times, but the current was far too strong for me to stay latched on.

Multiple times as I felt I couldn't hold my breath a second longer, I'd pop up out of the water, allowing me to take a deep breath, only to be plunged back under the water again.

I bounced off of more rocks than I could count. Some were harder hits than others. I did all I could to protect my head.

And I was thankful that my backpack was on tight because it certainly protected my back a few dozen times.

Suddenly I stopped bouncing off of rocks and was able to feel the ground with my paws. I quickly pushed off of the ground towards the surface. I needed air because I felt that any second I was about to take a giant gasp.

I popped out of the water and was able to take not only one, but three giant breaths of air. I was facing backwards, so I turned around quickly to see where I was going. I saw the open sky just as I went over the waterfall.

As I fell, I did my best to turn my body so I would land into the water paws first. Unfortunately the pressure of the falling water had other plans for me. I was tossed and turned as I fell.

I didn't actually feel the moment I fell in the water. All I knew was that I was suddenly surrounded by bubbles and I could feel the ground beneath my feet. I tried to jump, but nothing happened. I tried again, nothing.

I began to panic and tried pushing myself in every direction that I could. Nothing was working.

Out of pure panic, I just allowed my body to go limp and said a prayer.

ENTRY 22

I OPENED MY EYES and coughed up some water. I found myself laying on the ground, next to the river, on some small rocks and dirt.

The water was calm behind me. I couldn't hear the roar of the water or waterfall.

I slowly stood up, carefully taking inventory of my body to make sure nothing was cut or broken. I was a little sore here and there, but overall, I was shocked that I wasn't badly injured.

I walked over to a large rock and sat down to absorb what had just happened to me. I sat on the rock and cried. I didn't really have any thoughts going through my mind at that moment. I just felt this need to let it all out, as they say.

Once I pulled myself together, my mind started to race and I began to beat myself up mentally.

Why didn't you just take the easy route like everyone else does? Then you wouldn't have been stung by bees, almost died, and then got caught in a river where you could have drowned?

You don't even know what you are searching for. Maybe you're just wasting your time.

Maybe you're not meant to be the type of cat who makes his own path.

Maybe you should just settle for an easy life like most other cats do.

Maybe you are not as strong as you thought or hoped you were.

I started to question everything and even myself.

What am I really doing anyway? I'm supposed to find my calling, my purpose, my mission. And so far, I'm not anywhere closer to finding it than when I left New Hampshire.

Go home, Ryko. Just go home.

The last thought really hit me. The thing is, I wanted to go home. This whole journey, fighting and clawing my own path in the forest was just not for me. I hate to admit it, but at that moment, I gave up. I gave up on the journey.

And I gave up on myself.

I stood up and said out loud, "I'm ready to go home... I... Give... Up."

I looked around, trying to figure out which way I should go to try and find a town. I was sick and tired of being in the forest. I wanted nothing else than to be on a train, headed back to New Hampshire to see my mother and father.

I felt like I had failed them.

I felt like I had failed everyone I met on my journey.

I felt like I had failed myself.

With my head down, I began to walk, following the flow and pace of the now slow moving river.

After nearly an hour, I decided to stop and get a bite to eat. My energy was running low and I couldn't remember the last time I ate.

I sat down on the ground and reached up to my chest to undo the strap on my backpack.

Ummm... Oh cat spit.

My backpack. It's gone.

I put my paw on my head and just shook my head from left to right. "Seriously, what else could possibly go wrong!" I screamed.

"I give up, OK? You win! I'm not cut out for this. I just want to go home!"

I stood up. "I don't care about my backpack anyway," I said. And I continued to walk along the river.

As I walked, the memory of Kory running her paw through her hair slowly appeared in my mind. The feeling of missing her started to tug slightly on my stomach and heart.

"Kory's address. My journal. All my friends. My *Whisker Hollows* book. My parents. Oh no. I need my backpack." I turned around and followed my paw prints back to where I had washed up on the riverbank.

As I looked around, I noticed something strange that stopped me in my tracks. I bent down, next to where I had been lying just a few hours earlier, and right next to my own paw prints, were a set of other pawprints in the mud.

"Those are not my pawprints," I said to myself.

I stood up and thought for a moment. "Did someone take my backpack while I was laying here?"

I bent down and looked closer at the other paw prints. I walked around in circles, making a larger circle each time, trying to see if I could find another paw print.

Finally, after several minutes of searching, I found one. Then another and another. I followed the paw prints and they led to a trail in the forest.

I took a deep breath and followed them.

Hours had passed, and although at times I'd lose the trail of paw prints, I managed to find them again. It was getting dark, so I decided to call it a night.

I walked over to a large tree, curled up into a ball next to it, and fell asleep.

Now I'm the type of cat who rarely ever remembers his dreams. Maybe once a year, if I'm lucky, I'll have a dream that I remember. And that night happened to be one of those nights.

I was in New Hampshire, in my yard, playing cat ball with my father. We were having so much fun, laughing, and the weather was a perfect fall day. My mother was watching us, sipping on an iced apple cider, laughing, and cheering for both of us.

I remember my father tossed the ball and I batted it quickly. It went right past him, right into the goal. Everyone cheered.

As my father turned around to go get the ball out of the net, I was jumping up and down with my paws up in the air and I happened to look up into the sky.

I was captivated. The leaves were unlike anything I had ever seen. They were glistening in the sunlight. As I looked up in complete bewilderment of the sheer beauty of what I was seeing, I watched a leaf break free from a tree.

The leaf slowly fell down, back and forth, as it made its way to the ground. As the sunlight hit the leaf, small, colorful beams of light shot off of it. The colors were every color of a rainbow and more.

I reached out my paws, as the leaf gingerly landed in them. I drew the leaf to my face to get a better look. The leaf looked as if it was covered in millions of tiny pieces of glitter, each one taking in the sunlight and releasing its own glistening beam of light. I was in complete awe.

"Mother, father, come look at this!" I yelled. As I looked up at them, they weren't there. Nothing was there. And then I woke up.

ENTRY 23

BEFORE I STOOD UP, I sat at the base of the tree for several minutes recalling my dream. I remember each and every single detail like it just happened one minute ago. I remember every blade of grass. Every movement my mother and father made. The leaf with the rays of light. It all felt so real. It was such a surreal feeling.

I licked my paw, cleaned my ears, and stood up to get back onto the trail of the paw prints.

After several hours, I noticed that there was not one, but two sets of paw prints, and one set was quite fresh.

I bent down and put my paw print into the dirt next to the fresh paw print.

"Oh no," I said to myself. "Those are *my* paw prints."

Somehow, I ended up going in a circle following the other paw prints. All I could think of doing was going back and retracing my own steps.

I walked down the trail, making sure there were no other

paths or paw prints that I had missed before, that somehow got me off track.

After hours of following the trail, I was horrified by what I saw.

A third set of paw prints.

"No, no, this cannot be happening!" I yelled.

I slowly extended my paw to the first set of paw prints. "This one is definitely not mine," I said. I then put my paw by the next set of prints. "This is mine." And then to the final set of paw prints. "This is mine as well. How is this even possible!?" I yelled.

I sat for a moment to think of what to do, and then came up with an idea.

I took a few sticks and stood them up together in the middle of the path. "There. If I'm going in circles, I'll at least know where the circle starts." I scratched my head, wondering if my logic made any sense. I wasn't sure if it did. But at this point, I had no idea what else to do.

I began walking down the path. This time, very slowly, making absolutely sure there were no other paw prints leading off the path that I had missed the first, second, or I guess even third time I came through here.

As I walked, I kept my head down to the ground, scanning from side to side, ensuring nothing would get past me. Suddenly, I was startled by a bonk on my head.

I looked up and literally leapt back at what I saw.

It was the small structure of sticks I had made just minutes earlier.

"No, no no! I'm losing my mind!" I yelled. I sat down and looked up into the sky. I just didn't know what to do with myself.

I felt more defeated than I had ever felt in my life. I had given up on my journey. I had given up on myself. I had given up on my backpack, but the thoughts of Kory made me go back for it. But now I was regretting that decision.

I was starving.

I was lost.

I wanted to go home.

"What do you want from me!?" I yelled. "Are you happy now? You made me go crazy. I give up! You win! Is that what you want to hear!? I don't want to do this anymore. I don't want to do anything. I just want to go home!"

I fell to the ground. I had never felt more lost or more alone in my entire life. It was such an empty feeling.

Night fell, as I stayed seated on the ground.

ENTRY 24

AT THE FIRST SIGN OF SUNLIGHT, I stood up and started walking. I literally just got up and started walking straight. I didn't care about the paw prints. I just wanted out. I was done.

I could feel anger starting to run through my veins as I walked. My slight movements to move branches out of the way soon turned into outright lethal slashings by my paws, tearing branches and leaves to shreds.

I walked for hours. And I could tell it was nearly noon as the sun was directly above me.

As I was scanning my surroundings each step I took, something caught my eye in the distance. I wasn't quite sure what it was. Water? A pond? I just didn't know.

I began to run and found myself in a clearing that had a small field of grass. I slowed down as I moved towards what had caught my eye. And as I approached it, I could feel the hair start to stand up on the back of my neck.

I bent down, not believing my eyes. "This can't be real," I said to myself.

I extended my paw and picked up the leaf. It was the exact glistening leaf that I had just dreamed about.

As I studied the leaf, I felt the strangest sensation slowly wash over my body. It was warm, ran deep, and in many ways, was calming.

I slowly stood up and looked around.

This place was nothing like where I just was. Even the temperature was different. I turned around to look at the forest behind me and everything appeared normal. There was just something about this clearing.

The wind blew gently across the tall grass. It was so peaceful. I started walking forward and soon reached the end of the meadow. I turned to the right, looked down the treeline and spotted what appeared to be an entrance to a path.

As I walked, I held the leaf I was holding in the sunlight and watched the beams of light dance off of the leaf. I rubbed my paw across the top of the leaf to see what it felt like and it was as smooth as silk.

As I reached the path I noticed another leaf, just like the one I was holding in my hands, laying in the middle of the path.

I ran over to it, picked it up, and looked around. Then I looked back at the path in front of me.

The path was a straight line, down as far as the eye could see, and it was lined by white birch trees. I knew they were birch trees because we have them in New Hampshire, but I could tell that this place was nowhere near New Hampshire.

By this point, I had completely forgotten about the paw prints. And even my backpack. And for that matter, just about everything else.

I was just focused on these leaves and still awestruck by the fact that I had dreamed about the same leaf the night before. "How could this be? How is this possible?" I thought to myself.

After quite a long trek, the path ended. It literally just stopped being a path. There was no left, no right, and no turns to take.

I stood there for a moment, looking down at the two leaves in my paw. "I literally have nothing to lose," I said, as I walked past where the path had ended.

As I made my way through the incredibly dense forest, I don't know if I was in shock, in a trance of some sort, or if my mind just needed a break from all the stress. But I felt nothing. Literally nothing.

I don't recall a single thought going through my mind. I just made my way deeper into the forest. No real purpose. Just forward. Looking back on it now, it is clear that I was allowing my heart to guide me and I had finally got out of my own way.

As the sun began to go down, I reached an odd rock formation, which was in the center of a slightly rounded indentation in the ground.

I approached it and cautiously walked around the rocks sticking out of the ground. I couldn't tell if it was cat-made or just some random arrangement made by the forces of nature. I decided to hop onto one of the rocks and take a little break from walking.

Once on the top of the rock, I was surprised to see that the top was completely flat. Perfectly flat. "This truly looks like this has been worked on by the paws of cats," I said to myself. I leaned back onto the flat surface, sat down, and before I knew it, I drifted off to sleep.

ENTRY 25

I WAS SURPRISED TO WAKE UP and realize it was the next day. But that surprise was nothing compared to the surprise I got when I sat up.

As I looked down by my legs, I saw that there were leaves perfectly placed, outlining where I had been laying. I looked behind me, and the outline went all the way around where my head had been.

I picked up a leaf and saw it was just like the glistening leaves I had found.

I quickly jumped up and looked around. Obviously, I'm not alone here. And whoever is messing with me probably also has my backpack.

"Hello?" I said out loud. "You can stop messing with me now. I know you are out there. I just want my backpack back, and then I will be on my way."

I walked in tight circles on the flat rock, looking all around me, as I tried to spot any movement in the forest.

"I'm tired of these games, What do you want from me?" I yelled. There was silence.

I jumped down from the rock and decided to explore the area a little. I walked around, looking for paw prints or any other signs of someone else and came up empty.

"Show yourself!" I yelled, as I walked back to the rock.

I jumped back on top of the rock, sat down, and scanned the area around me. For the first time in quite awhile, I had time to think clearly about this entire situation.

By that point, I was pretty convinced, nearly certain, that I had truly and completely fallen off my rocker. Yup. I was nuts. Bonkers. Gone crazy. I mean seriously, this type of stuff does not happen, right? I mean come on.

As I sat, scanning my surroundings and determining what level of crazy I'd reached, I was snapped out of it by a noise.

I quickly crouched down with my ears pointing in the direction of the noise. My back legs were moving back and forth, as my tail swooshed from side to side. I was ready to pounce at any second.

The noise became louder and was repeating. Paw steps!

I ducked down as low as I could.

Suddenly, a very old cat appeared from behind a tree. He was wearing a large backpack and had a walking stick in his left paw. In his right paw there appeared to be a stack of the glistening leaves.

He could see me. I could see him. We locked eyes. I didn't move one muscle. Neither did he. The tension in the air was unlike anything I had ever felt. I didn't know if I should pounce the old cat or just stand my ground.

Several absolutely intense minutes went by.

Then, the old cat made his move.

He stuck his walking stick out in front of him and placed one end to the ground. He then took a step forward, towards me.

I felt my muscles tighten in my shoulders, as I prepared for battle.

Then a moment later, the old cat moved his other paw and took another step towards me.

I took a slow, deep breath and tried to recall all the moves my father taught me when we used to play fight. Then another moment passed and the old cat moved his walking stick ahead again, followed by one paw forward, a moment after.

This time I felt the tenseness of my muscles begin to release. I remember thinking, "I bet he's going to move the next paw forward."

And a moment later, he did.

This process continued for nearly twenty minutes. By the time my body was completely relaxed, I somehow found some humor in this slow-motion standoff of sorts. However, we never took our eyes off each other. And neither of us blinked that I can recall.

Finally, about thirty feet or so from the rock I was sitting on, he stopped his forward progress, which, to be honest, I was grateful for. At the rate he was going, we were going to be there all night and he was going to have to witness me go number two while staring into his eyes. And that would have been weird and really awkward. When you gotta go, you gotta go.

"Ryko," the old cat said in a stern voice.

I remained silent but actually felt a huge relief for a couple of reasons. For one, this old cat either had my backpack or knew me from somewhere. And two, he probably knew a way out of this crazy place.

"Yeah?" I replied. Then I second-guessed myself whether I should have admitted who I was right off the bat.

"I mean, maybe I am. Or maybe I'm not," I said.

"You going to help an old cat make it over to that rock?" he said, as he raised his walking stick. "Or are you just going to watch me take forever and a day to make it all the way over there?"

The tension that previously felt as though it could be cut with a knife suddenly felt more like a deflated balloon.

I hopped down off the rock and moved toward the old cat.

I could see he could do absolutely zero harm to me. His eyes were kind and gentle and as blue as the bluest of skies. His fur was nearly all white, minus a few specks of gray here and there.

And he had a long beard that had some grass stuck to the bottom of it.

As I moved closer, I immediately could sense his presence. I have never, and I mean never sensed anything like what he had. Cats are very good at sensing things. Danger, the moves of others, feelings of others, and all sorts of things. But what I sensed from this old cat was something greater than I have ever felt. There are no words to describe the feeling.

"You've come a long way," the old cat said, as he looked at me and then off into the distance.

The entire mood of the situation morphed into something entirely different as each second passed. I don't know how I knew, but I could feel I was in the presence of someone or something extremely special, rare, and almost sacred. I almost felt the urge to bow, but shook that off and tried to remind myself that I had come to the conclusion that I was officially crazy.

I walked up to the old cat and didn't say a word. I offered my shoulder and helped him over to the rock, where he took a seat. I took a seat on the ground in front of him.

As I looked up at the old cat, the sun was perfectly behind his head. Because of the angle of the sun and his fur, there was a light, almost like a halo around his entire head.

I could feel something happening inside of me. I didn't know what. I just knew that all, and I mean literally all, of the negative thoughts and feelings that had been growing inside of me over the past several weeks had completely dissipated.

The feelings that were washing over me was similar to the feelings and sensations you feel during a very deep catnap. However, my eyes were wide open, just looking at this old cat. I felt completely zoned and dialed in.

The old cat put the glistening leaves down on his left side, as they continued to cast colorful rays of light from the sunlight. Then he proceeded to remove his large backpack and set it on the ground in front of him.

His movements were methodical, smooth, and somehow had an extremely calming effect over me. He reached over to the zipper on the top of his backpack and slowly unzipped it all the way until the backpack was completely open.

He proceeded to take out my backpack and placed it on the ground next to his. Then he looked down at me with his sparkling blue eyes.

"Lost are those who have tied their own knot. Free are those who cut the rope in the beginning."

The old cat just looked at me. I wasn't sure if he was waiting for me to respond or exactly what was happening.

"I don't understand," I said.

"To find self, one must get lost. To get lost, one must lose self," the old cat said, as he nodded.

I broke eye contact as my eyes wandered around, trying to absorb what the old cat said. I thought to myself, "Obviously, I'm lost. I think I may have lost myself because I went crazy. Maybe I am still crazy. Who knows, maybe none of this is real and I'm imagining all of it. This is just a lot for a cat to handle, you know."

I looked at the old cat. I felt it would be best for me to sound like him, so I said, "For me, lost. For me, went crazy. For me, lost backpack. Backpack... now found?"

The old cat didn't look pleased and slowly squinted his eyes at me.

"Come," the old cat said as he stood up from the rock and zipped up his backpack.

ENTRY 26

FOR AN OLD CAT who needed help walking over to the rock, he somehow got a boost of energy or something. I was having trouble keeping up with him even without my backpack.

We walked into the night silently. The only light we had was that of the moon, which was in and out of the clouds, making seeing where we were going very difficult at times.

As we walked, I tried to make out something, anything of my surroundings, and it was nearly impossible. At one point, I thought I could see mountains in the distance, but I soon realized it was only clouds.

The forest was dense, but we remained on a fairly straight and flat path the entire time. I was grateful for that, as I truly had enough bushwhacking for a very long time.

In an instant, the clouds completely covered the moon. Thankfully I could see a little, but us cats need at least a tiny bit of light to see in the dark. There was barely any light and I could see maybe five feet in front of me, just enough to follow the old cat.

He finally stopped and pointed to a large square rock in front of us. "Sit," he said.

I walked over to the rock and sat down. He just stood in front of me.

I looked around and could tell that the trail was in front of me. There were trees not too far off to my left. There was a very large tree to my right that I could reach out and touch with my paw. And behind me, well, I turned around, and it was just pitch black. I had no idea what was behind me.

And the air. Something was different about the air from where we had just come from.

I turned back toward where the old cat was standing. He was gone.

"Stay. Sleep," the old cat's voice said in the distance.

I sat there for quite a while, thinking about everything that just transpired. "Things have gone from great to amazing, to bad to horrible, to confusing to scary, to now I don't know what." I thought. As I sat there, I made a decision.

I decided to stop trying to figure everything out. I was going to drive myself crazy, possibly again. I decided that I had nothing, literally nothing, to lose from just going with the flow to seeing what unfolds. I felt a little sense of peace with my decision.

I curled up in a ball, closed my eyes, and went to sleep.

ENTRY 27

As the sunlight warmed my body and the light woke me up, I stretched my arms and legs. Oh that felt good, but also a little strange. As I placed my legs and arms back where they were, I felt something under them and heard a soft crunch.

I opened my eyes to see what was on me as the beams of the glistening leaves casted the light upon my face. I could feel that the leaves were all around me and there were several on top of me.

"This old cat is a little crazy with these glistening leaves," I thought to myself. "He keeps putting them on me and he carries them around with him. How odd."

I heard footsteps in the distance and opened my eyes wider. The old cat was walking towards me.

"Sit up. Face me," he said in a rather stern voice.

I did what he said. He placed his backpack on the ground, unzipped it, removed my backpack again, and placed it next to his.

I clearly remember thinking, "Oh no, here we go again."

He sat down behind our backpacks and looked at me intensely.

"Close your eyes," the old cat said.

I noticed that he didn't have his walking stick with him, so I felt pretty confident that I wasn't going to get bonked in the head with it. I listened to him with my eyes closed.

"What is it you seek?" The old cat asked.

I thought for a moment and tried to figure out where he was going with this. The first answer that popped into my head was, "my backpack", but I had a feeling it was the wrong answer and might result in him zipping it up and playing this game again tomorrow.

I thought about saying, "A way back home", but felt that wasn't the answer he wanted to hear either. And then it hit me. The whole reason why I was at that very spot at that very moment.

"I seek my purpose. My mission. My calling," I said out loud.

"And where do you suppose you will find what you seek?" the old cat asked.

The first thing that came to mind was that if I knew what my calling was I wouldn't be here. But I took my time and thought deeper. Although I didn't understand my answer, it's one I've always known. It's just something that has always eluded me.

I cleared my throat and answered, "Inside of myself,"

The old cat then asked, "What is it inside of you, Ryko?"

As I sat there, I came up blank. What was inside of me? Deep down, I felt the old cat was referring to that one thing that had eluded me my entire life. That one feeling. That one thing that I could never put my paw on.

I started asking myself over and over, "What's inside of me? What's inside of me? What's inside of me?"

As I asked this question, I thought about my life. Visions of my childhood appeared. I was playing. I was happy. And then I saw my parents. They were hugging me and taking care of me. Then I saw Kory. I remembered how I felt when she put her head on my chest and I put my arm around her.

A tear ran down my face.

"Love. It's love that is inside of me," I said softly.

Multiple tears started to stream down my face. For the first time in my life, I finally put a word to that feeling that had been living inside of me that I could not put my paws on. But it wasn't just love. No, it was even more powerful and more special than any love I could give to anyone.

It was the love that I had for myself.

So that's what I said out loud, "It is the love I have for myself."

I could hear the old cat get up and some rustling around, but I continued to keep my eyes closed. I could literally feel my heart and soul open and I felt boundless love pouring into me, as I allowed my boundless love to pour out.

The old cat began to speak:

Rustling stars; prevailing breeze,

Yearning for more, missing keys.

Kindred spirit; ineffable desire,

Only love can ignite the fire.

My eyes sprang open. "That is my favorite poem! I know these words like the back of my hand!" I thought to myself.

I looked up at the old cat and softly said, "Only love can ignite the fire."

The old cat was holding my *Whisker Hollows* book open to the last page, where the poem was.

He turned the book around towards me and pointed his paw to the word "Rustling" and looked at me. I said, "Rustling," and he shook his head and pointed his paw again.

"R," I said. He then moved his paw to the next line. "Y," I said. And then he moved to the next line. "K," I said as I started to breathe quickly, I could barely see past the tears in my eyes.

The old cat pointed to the last word. "O," I said. "RYKO." I had literally lost my breath. I was frozen. I had no thoughts. No movement. I just sat there, bewildered.

The old cat turned the book back around and then read the last passage out loud.

Sacred stone; soft rolling hills,
Glistening leaves, water fulfills.
Sacred knowledge; ancient clues,
Follow your heart it's time to choose.

The old cat bent down on one knee and looked right into my eyes.

"Sacred stone." He placed his paw on the rock I was sitting on.

"Soft rolling hills." He extended his paw behind me.

"Glistening leaves" He pointed to the leaves and tree next to me.

"Water fulfills." He pointed behind me again.

"Sacred knowledge." He placed his paw on the book and then to his head.

"Ancient clues." He placed his paw over his heart.

"Follow your heart." He placed his paw over my heart.

"It's time to choose." The old cat stood up and motioned his paws for me to look behind me.

I slowly turned my head, and what I saw completely and fully overwhelmed each and every single cell in my body with pure love, awe, and amazement

I stood up to absorb the majestic beauty that was in front of me. The old cat walked up and stood beside me.

"Welcome to Whisker Hollows," he said in a soft, tender voice.

I looked over at the old cat. I took a deep breath and swallowed hard as I wiped tears from my face. "York?" I asked.

The old cat turned and looked off in the distance. "Yes," he answered.

ENTRY 28

I WAS SO WRAPPED UP by what I was looking at, I didn't notice York had left my side.

I had never come close to feeling the sense of bewilderment I did at that very moment, as I looked out upon Whisker Hollows. I always had a feeling or some sort of knowing that this was a real place. And it was.

"How is this even possible? How am I somehow a part of this? What is the meaning of all of this?" Questions like these and thousands of others danced around my head.

I looked on the rock I had been sitting on and there it was. "Whisker Hollows" was carved into the rock, just as York had described. And the tree by the rock, was none other than the majestic oak tree that towered into the sky and was covered in glistening leaves.

As I looked up at the tree and a few leaves fell with the breeze onto the rock, I realized that York didn't place those glistening leaves on me last night. They fell from the tree.

I turned back around, closed my eyes, and took a deep breath of the crisp, sweet air. I knew the air was different when I arrived, but now I could actually taste the air. I opened my eyes and tried again to soak in everything I was seeing.

Where I stood, where the "Whisker Hollows" carved rock and majestic oak tree sit, is on top of a hill. The hill, covered in green and golden grass, rolled slowly down a long way, gently to a very large valley.

At the bottom of the valley, there was a beautiful lake that sparkled unlike any other lake I have ever seen. The water literally sparkled like diamonds.

There were a handful of trees, scattered throughout the valley. Each and every single one glistened in the sunlight, with rays of multi-colored lights shining off their leaves.

There were many rolling hills in the valley, blanketed by the golden and green grass like the one that the rock and majestic oak tree stood on.

In the far distance there was a forest that surrounded the entire valley which led to steep mountains that shot up into the sky. They were so tall that there was snow on the tops of them. I never saw clouds in the sky, but I would bet that the tops of the mountains would extend far above the clouds.

The air had a slightly sweet and crisp taste to it. It reminded me a little of the air in New Hampshire, during the fall, when you walk through apple orchards on a cool, windy, and cloudy fall day. Being there made me want to take in deep breaths because the air itself was so calming.

And the feeling I got as I allowed my eyes to soak in the beauty of Whisker Hollows was exactly as York described in his book. I felt a deep happiness that started in the center of my chest and radiated down throughout my body, from the top of my head down to my paws.

I felt empowered, like I could do anything, and that anything and everything was possible. I could see why York said that this is the place where dreams go to come true. I don't see how anything couldn't come true here.

The first wish I made was that my Mom and Dad could come to Whisker Hollows and see that it is real. After all, they read the *Whisker Hollows* book hundreds of times over the years. They knew the book and story as well as I did. I could only imagine the looks on their faces if they actually got to experience Whisker Hollows for themselves.

I called out for York, but he didn't answer and I just couldn't resist. I had to get down to the valley to see what it was like down by the lake.

I walked down the rolling hills. Through tall grass and short grass. Up and down, ever so gently. As I walked, a cool breeze rolled through the valley making the grass in the distance sway into beautiful patterns.

I've done my best to avoid using this word to describe Whisker Hollows, but as I walked closer to the lake, I couldn't help it... It just felt magical. I noticed some sparkly purple rocks on the ground and picked one up to take a look at it.

It was unlike rock I had ever seen. It was almost like a jewel. I held it up to the sun and the rock had tiny little beams of purple light shining out of it. As I inspected the rock closer, it looked like it had the same type of material inside it that was on the leaves.

Once I got to the water, it was as if I was looking at millions upon millions of small diamonds, all dancing in harmony, making small waves. I reached my paw into the water. It felt like normal water. I bent down and took a small sip. It was delicious! It tasted like normal water, but with a little added sweetness.

I walked over to a few trees that were nearby. They were obviously oak trees, as they were the same type of tree by the rock up on the hill. As I walked towards the trees, I could see there was something on one of them.

I walked up to the tree to inspect it and found a strange symbol carved into it.

From afar, the symbol sort of looked like a dragonfly. But as I got closer to it, I noticed there were a lot of details. Squiggly lines, some dots, and some weird shapes. I had absolutely no clue what I was looking at.

I continued to explore for a few hours and decided to head back up to the majestic oak tree on the hill to see if York was there.

I walked through the tall grass, with both paws extended out to my sides, tilted my head up, and walked slowly, absorbing the magnificence. I felt like I was on top of the world, so full of happiness and love.

As I got closer to the oak tree on the hill, I could see York sitting on the rock.

"Hi York," I said as I made my way to the top. York nodded.

"I realize it is only natural for you to have many questions, Ryko," York said. "But you must release them. Let what meows, meow."

I sat down in the grass in front of York, who was looking out into the valley. He held his walking stick and his backpack was on the ground beside the rock. He looked proud, at peace, and had a sense of such inner calmness about him.

"I have spent seven of my lives here, Ryko. Whisker Hollows holds not just secrets and knowledge, but keys. And not just keys, *the key*."

York turned towards me and looked at me with his kind, ocean blue eyes. "Time is neutral. It doesn't care either way. Whether you come, whether you go, or whether you stay. But in your case, Ryko, just as the prophecy states, *it's time to choose*."

I let what York said sit within me for a moment. "The poem, you mean," I said.

York smiled. "Follow your heart Ryko," he said softly.

I looked around for a moment, then back up to York. "I'm going to listen to what you say and not ask questions, which let me tell you, is really hard, almost impossible, for me to do right now. But I will do the best I can. Now obviously there is some connection here with me, Whisker Hollows, maybe you, and my purpose. So the poem, or prophecy, or whatever it is, says that it's my time to choose?" I asked while scratching my chin.

York sat silent so I took that as the okay for me to continue. "What I'm struggling to wrap my head around is exactly what it is that I'm choosing. I thought my journey, or really anyone's journey, is to find our purpose. I didn't know there was a choice. I always thought you just somehow found it," I said as I struggled to make sense of my own words and what York was saying to me.

York leaned in towards me. "Trust your heart, Ryko. You already know the answer. Speak your wishes into the air."

I thought for a moment and remembered what I've told my parents for as long as I could remember. I thought about the untold number of times my parents told me that I was here to make a positive difference in this world. I remembered the countless conversations I had with myself in the forest in New Hampshire, as I tried to figure this whole puzzle out. And I remember what I told Kory.

I looked up at York and said, "I am here to make a real difference. To have a positive impact on the lives of cats all around the world. To make cats smile, laugh, and love. To play a role in helping cats get rescued and adopted. And to leave a loving paw print on the hearts of many."

As the words were coming out of my mouth, I was surprised at how I strung them together. I'd always had pieces, but I had never voiced it in such a concise way before.

York took his walking stick and began to write on the ground. He drew a big "H," followed by an "O," and then a "W."

York stood up, picked up his backpack, put it on, and started walking down the trail. "Catnap for the answer," York said, as he disappeared into the woods.

ENTRY 29

I SAT ON THE ROCK with my legs crossed, facing Whisker Hollows. I placed my paws on my lap and closed my eyes.

1...2...3...4... I took a deep breath in. 4...3...2...1... I breathed out. I continued this process as I watched the stream of tens of thousands of thoughts fly by me in rapid succession. I remained present and allowed the thoughts to pass by me and eventually through me. I allowed them to flow by without grabbing onto one.

As the stream of thoughts faded, an image of a trail appeared in my mind's eye. I remained still. Once the stream of thoughts were completely gone, I began to walk down the trail.

It was familiar. The trees and the leaves were all glistening. I continued walking and saw the majestic oak tree and rock ahead. As I approached them, I saw myself sitting on the rock, catnapping.

I observed myself and then looked out upon the valley. Instead of a handful of glistening trees, there was a bustling town in the distance, with even more glistening trees all around it.

I could make out a small downtown area with shops and small buildings that were surrounded by multiple houses and farms in the distance by the lake. Then, a little further, there was a very large white building with something written on the side of it that I couldn't quite make out.

As I observed the town, I could see movement. Cats were moving from one place to the next. They all had a purpose, some sort of big mission. A very important one I felt.

The moment I took a step further, the image began to slowly fade. And then there was complete darkness followed by light as I gradually opened my eyes.

I took a few deep breaths and was a bit taken back by my experience. I started to question everything, but I quickly muted those questions and said to myself, "Let what meows, meow."

I looked down at the ground at the word, "How" that York had drawn onto the ground. I let this sit within me as I stood up. "Let's see where York went," I said.

As I walked into the forest where York entered, I followed a small winding trail and spotted what appeared to be multiple huts in the distance. I walked towards the huts and saw there was light coming out of one with a little bit of smoke rising from the chimney.

I walked up the small path which led to a few stairs and then knocked on the door.

"Welcome," York said as he opened the door, abruptly turned around, and walked away.

Assuming that meant York was welcoming me inside his house, I slowly walked inside, shutting the door rather loudly behind me, announcing that I was inside, in a not-so-subtle way.

I really didn't have any expectations nor any thoughts about where York lived. Inside was incredibly simple. There was a small bed located to the left of the door. To the right was a wood stove and a small table with two chairs. Further in was another chair to the left that looked like a homemade rocking chair and what I assumed was the kitchen to the right. Finally, off the kitchen was a hallway leading to who knows where.

"Come in. Sit, sit," York said as he came out of the hallway and put on a pair of old glasses. I decided to sit in the chair, closest to the kitchen. York walked over to the stove and placed what looked like carrots or some orange food into a pot and put a cover on it.

Then York took two cups out of a small cupboard and scooped what appeared to be a green powder into them. He reached towards the stove, picked up a tea kettle, and poured hot water into the cups.

"Wrong choice," York said as he walked by me, carrying the two cups of what I assumed was tea and went over to the table by the woodstove.

I got up, walked to the other table, and sat down.

"Look," I said. "I completely understand the whole, 'let what meows, meow' thing. I really do. And there are questions I have, probably hundreds of them I'd guess, just sitting in the back of my mind that I am ignoring. But there are some serious questions I need to ask you."

York took a sip of his tea, looked up at me, and smiled. "Serious questions are the questions one should ask."

I put my paw on the cup and quickly realized that it was still too hot for me to touch. "The first serious question I have is, why me? You wrote the book years, I guess a few decades before I was even born. How do you know I'm *the* Ryko?"

"That is not for me to decide," York replied quickly.

"OK, I'm going to shelf that question and try to figure that one out later. Now, I had this vision, a vivid dream, whatever you want to call it, on the rock earlier. I saw a town in the valley of Whisker Hollows. There were cats working down there and a large building in the distance. Is there any sort of connection with all of this here, or am I just dreaming, or..." I asked.

"That is not for me to decide," York replied without hesitation.

I let out a big sigh. "OK, I see what is going on here. So what about this place? Where you live? What are the other houses for? Are there others that live here?"

York was midway to lift his tea to meet his mouth for a sip, but then slowly put the cup down and looked up at me.

"Long before I arrived here, there was an ancient civilization that resided here. I'd dedicated many of my lives searching and even finding many of their secrets and hidden wisdom. And there are many of them. Where those who were here long before me went, I do not know." York reached for his tea and took another sip.

I reached for mine and the cup was still too hot. I was thirsty and maybe a little frustrated that I still couldn't take a sip. "So why the book? Why did you write it? And why was it taken away shortly after it was published?" I asked.

"To plant the seed," York answered, "Seed was planted. And there was no more need for the seeds."

I leaned back in my chair to absorb what York had said. I was starting to realize that this was something I needed to get used to when talking to York."

After a few moments I decided to ask, "What wisdom or secrets have you found in Whisker Hollows?"

As York looked straight at me it was if he was looking right into me. It was an intense feeling.

York ran his paw through his long, white beard. "Now that, Ryko, is a very serious question." He paused for a moment, never taking his eyes off of me. I had to look away multiple times because I could literally feel the tension in my head. "They have the power to bring countless laughs to kittens, an untold number of smiles to adult cats, and happiness to all who are exposed to them."

I broke my newly formed rule to stop and think before I spoke to York and quickly said, "Wait. I have always felt those things. That it was somehow my mission to make that happen. It's what my parents have told me since I was a kitten. It was the feeling I felt all the time in the pit of my stomach and in my heart. I know with every hair on my body that there has to be a connection here. I mean it's obvious, right?" I paused for a few seconds, sighed, and continued. "My wild and crazy journey somehow led me here. I almost died a couple of times. I gave up on my journey, mission, and even myself, a few times. And yes, I may have even gone a little crazy a time or two as well. But I mean, look at this. Look at all of this. It all makes so much sense. It's all connected. Literally, all of it. Whisker Hollows has always been a huge part of my life. I've always felt it. I've always known it."

York listened to me intently and didn't move a muscle. In fact, I don't think he even blinked once during my little speech.

There was more, so much more I wanted to say, but I kept my mouth shut. I had a feeling York was waiting for me to finish my little rant. He continued to look right into me.

"Rustling stars; prevailing breeze," York said firmly. He paused for a few seconds, then continued, "Yearning for more, missing keys."

"Yearning for more," I said. "That's me. Always feeling like there is something more, something bigger." I paused for a few seconds. "And missing keys. The missing keys are the secrets and hidden knowledge here at Whisker Hollows."

I thought about the entire poem in the back of the *Whisker Hollows* book. One of the next lines kept repeating in my head. The same line we spoke earlier.

"York," I said, looking down at my cup of tea. "Only love can ignite the fire." I took a deep breath and paused.

I looked at York in the eyes and said, "It's what we were talking about earlier. There is another side to it. "It's not only the love inside of me igniting the fire within myself, it's also the love of others I need to ignite. Somehow I need to create something that ignites everyone's fire, so it spreads love."

York leaned in closer and softly asked, "How?"

I was expecting something more from York. A high five? A little dance? Something. I thought I had figured out the big missing piece of the puzzle, only to be led back to the "How?" question.

York stood up from the table as he drank the last of his tea. I reached out to my cup and immediately pulled back my paw. Ouch. The cup is still too hot. York must have paws of steel.

"Sleep now," York said, as he walked to the door.

I stood up and walked to the door as York opened it. I walked outside, paused for a few seconds, just when another question popped into my head. I went to open my mouth to speak right when York closed the door. I walked back up to the rock by the majestic oak tree with only one word on my mind: How?

ENTRY 30

I AWOKE IN ABSOLUTE SHEER PANIC and terror as the sun was just starting to come up. Smoke. I smelled smoke. And lots of it.

I started coughing and gagging, ran to York's house, and pounded on the door.

"Fire! Fire!" I screamed. York opened the door and just stood there.

"York, there's a big fire, I don't know if it's Whisker Hollows or what. What do we do?"

York walked to the side of the woodstove, got his walking stick, put on his backpack, and came back to the door.

"No fire." York said calmly. "But it's time to go to the rock anyway."

I ran ahead of York, but he was walking much slower than usual. I ran back down to him, and then decided to run up to the rock, expecting to see a blazing fire in the distance or closeby.

When I arrived at the rock, I saw nothing but the beauty that

Whisker Hollow contains. I took a deep breath in through my nose. The only thing I could smell was the crisp, sweet air of Whisker Hollows.

I walked over and sat on the rock, confused. I knew that wasn't a dream. I literally inhaled the smoke. I know I did because I was coughing and gagging as I ran to York's house. I don't understand.

York finally made it up to the rock.

"No fire." York said calmly as he bent over, unzipped his backpack, and took out my backpack.

He stood up, looked me deep into my eyes, and held out my backpack with his paw.

I reached up, took it from him, and then I put it on.

York motioned for me to sit, so I sat on the ground. He took his usual spot on the rock.

York looked into the distance and up towards the soaring mountains. After a long period of silence, York said, "The journey is both down and up."

This seemed obvious to me. Of course there are ups and downs. That's life. But knowing York, there was another meaning behind this. I thought about what he said for a while and then I had a hunch.

I took off my backpack and unzipped it. As I did, I could see York's head turns towards me.

I took out the *Whisker Hollows* book and flipped to the last page. I read the poem down, as I have a thousand times. And then I read the poem back up. I felt my heart sink, but I wasn't sure why.

York took his walking stick and pointed to the word, "HOW" he had scraped into the ground. "It will come, but you must go," York said.

York slowly stood up, looked over at me, put his hand on my shoulder, winked, and then walked towards the forest.

"Go as in leave Whisker Hollows?" I asked. "Go as in to the valley? Go where?"

I stood up and watched York disappear into the forest.

"Home." I said to myself. "It's time to go home."

ENTRY 31

I DON'T KNOW HOW it's even possible. Heck, I don't know how any of this is possible, but getting out of Whisker Hollows only took an hour of walking down perfectly fine trails.

When the trail ended, I found myself on a road. I looked behind me, and the giant mountains of Whisker Hollows were nowhere to be seen. "Figures," I said. "But I know for sure that this was all real."

I took off my backpack and unzipped the first pocket. I reached in and pulled out the purple rock that I had picked up in the Whisker Hollows valley. I held it up to the sun and watched the purple beams of light shimmer off of the rock. I put it back in my backpack, zipped it up, put it on, and began walking down the road.

I had no idea what state I was in, but the air had a bit of a nip to it. As I looked up at the trees, I saw that the leaves were changing to bright reds, yellows, and oranges. Fall was in the air.

It took me a few days, but I finally made it to a train station and got a ticket to New Hampshire.

While I was on the train, I had my first real opportunity in, I don't know how long, to ponder. And in many ways, I had no idea where to even start. My journey had taken me on so many unexpected twists and turns that I didn't even know what to think.

I began to imagine how my conversation with my mother and father might go. Do I tell them about Whisker Hollows first? Do I tell them about Kory first? About my backpack getting stolen? About the other amazing cats I met on my journey? About the bees? The waterfall? The amazing chocolate milk? I honestly had no idea where to even start.

But there was one thing that I knew for sure. I had better figure out the "How" as soon as I could. That was really, in many ways, my final missing piece of the puzzle. I thought to myself, "If I haven't figured it out by the time I get home, maybe my mother and father will have some ideas."

As the train rolled through the countryside, I reached into my backpack and took out my journal. I opened an empty page and started writing about my journey. I thought maybe writing everything that has happened to me would help me with my "How."

After all, there is no possible way I'm going to remember everything that has happened on my journey a month from now, let alone a few days from now. Everything is just far too important to forget. I mean, if we don't document our own journey, what stories will we have to share?

As I wrote in my journal, I paused to look out the window. Looking back, there were so many important lessons I learned. So many things that happened at the time seemed small, even meaningless, but without those tiny moments, the big picture could never be painted.

"Next stop, New Hampshire," said a voice over the speakers in my railcar.

"Wow, that was fast," I said under my breath.

I packed up my things and waited for the train to stop. I was excited. There was literally nothing in the world that I wanted more than a long, warm hug from my mother and father. I had a big smile on my face. I felt happy.

The train came to a stop, I jumped off, and began the walk home. My walk quickly turned into a jog, as I thought about my mother and father, and of course, warm apple cake!

ENTRY 32

I ran up the steep hill on Pleasant Street. Franklin looked the same as it always has. I took a deep breath of the fresh fall air. I looked up at the trees covered in bright orange, yellow, and red leaves dancing in the breeze.

I couldn't help but think of the glistening leaves of Whisker Hollows. Then it dawned on me that I should have packed a leaf in my backpack to show to my mother and father, but at least I had the purple rock. I knew they had never seen anything like that before. I know I never have.

My jog turned into a fast walk as I caught my breath and turned onto Terrace road. Mr. Woodcat was outside raking leaves in his large yard and whistling, as he always did. He was a much older cat, but somehow he never seemed to age. He looked the same as he did when I was a kitten.

I remember a few years back I used to sneak into his garden and pick strawberries. He caught me only two times and thankfully he never told my parents.

As I walked by his big yard, he happened to look up while he raked a giant pile of leaves into a bag. The moment he saw me, he froze. I smiled, waved, and yelled, "Hello Mr. Woodcat!"

He didn't move a muscle. I thought that was very odd. I looked straight ahead a few more steps and then looked back at Mr. Woodcat. He had turned towards me and continued to stare at me.

So weird. I shrugged it off and turned my head back to the road in front of me. I had a few more houses to go. Just the thought of being home gave me a burst of energy, and I started running.

Three more houses... Two more houses... I can see my driveway... and I made it!

I made a sharp turn right and headed down my dirt driveway. "Mother! Father!" I yelled, as I ran.

"I'm... home?"

My run came to a complete standstill.

My entire body went numb.

I took one tiny step forward. And then another.

"Nooooooooooo!" I cried out, as I ran to what was left of our house.

"Mother! Father!" I screamed.

There wasn't much left.

A fire had reduced nearly everything to a pile a black dust.

It was silent. There wasn't even a bird chirping, which I don't recall ever happening. It was so quiet that I could hear my own heart pounding.

I walked up to where the front door had once stood. My eyes instantly welled up with tears, which began to flow down both my cheeks.

I continued to walk on the ground where our home once stood. Just two single boards from the door frame remained standing where the front of our home was. To my right, there was nothing. The wall, pictures, kitchen table, cabinets, gone. All gone.

Straight ahead was a wall that still stood with a window. The glass was all missing. The kitchen sink was lying sideways on the ground. There was a small pile against the wall by the sink, which I assumed was what used to be our refrigerator.

To my left was a wall that partially still stood, as well as a badly burned cabinet. All of my mother's photos and books that were on top of the cabinet were reduced to ash.

I took several steps forward, passed the cabinet and looked left, down what used to be the hallway where my parents' room and my room once were. There was nothing. No walls. Literally, nothing was left standing.

I walked over to where my room once was, and the only thing recognizable were a few black springs on the ground, which I knew were from my bed.

As I surveyed my surroundings, I felt completely numb. I could feel tears dripping down my face, but I had no feeling in my body. There were little to zero thoughts going through my head. I was in complete shock.

The smell of burned wood filled the air.

I walked back over to the half burned cabinet that was against one of the remaining walls. I reached for the handle of the one remaining door, grabbed it with my paw, and the door fell to the ground and made a giant ash cloud.

I coughed and swatted the air in front of my face with my paw. Once the ash cloud cleared, I bent down to look inside the blackened space.

I knew this cabinet well. This was where my parents kept all the important papers we had. It had the papers for the land, the house, papers that were important to my mother and father, and all of the drawings I had made since I was a kitten.

Inside, there was a large pile of ash. I looked on the ground and saw a large metal spike that must have been from the roof. It was quite bent from the heat of the fire.

I picked the spike up and poked it into the pile of ash inside the cabinet and struck something hard. I poked it a little more and could tell that I was hitting something made out of tin or metal. I dropped the spike and reached inside, delicately moving the ash with my paw.

There was a slight reflection from the sunlight on what looked like the corner of the object. I reached right in with both paws, got a hold of what I could now tell was a box, and carefully took it out.

There was a pile of ash several inches thick on the top of it and I walked back out the door frame, and into the grass. I tilted the box, allowing the ashes to fall onto the grass. This exposed the burned, but still partially readable logo for Wildlife Binoculars.

It was then I completely lost it.

I fell to my knees, meowed, and cried harder than any cat has ever cried. At least an hour passed, maybe two.

I had no more tears left to cry. My eyes were swollen, dry, and my entire body ached unlike anything I had ever felt. This hurt like one million bee stings at once.

I moved my legs out in front of me and sat down and looked over at the burned Wildlife Binoculars metal box. I remembered how just two years prior, my parents got me this for my birthday so I could look at the birds, squirrels, and whatever else on my, "Great journeys into Whisker Hollows," I would say, as I'd go play in the woods behind our house.

I had always loved that box. It used to have "Wildlife Binoculars" in large white letters on the top and an image of three cats looking out over a lake and up at the mountains with the binoculars up to their faces. Now all that was left was a little bit of red paint on the bottom left corner and only a part of the name on the top.

As I picked up the box, I tried to remember what I had put in it and then remembered that I had given it to my mother awhile back to put her fancy silverware in.

The box felt very light as I set it down onto my lap. There was definitely no silverware inside. I attempted to open it but failed. As

I tilted it onto its side to try another angle, I heard and felt something shift inside.

After several more futile attempts, it wouldn't budge. I took off my backpack, unzipped it, and placed the tin inside.

ENTRY 33

My slight knocks turned into hard bangs on the door. Even though Mr. or Mrs. Woodcat's bikes weren't on the bike rack by the door, I kept knocking and soon scratching at the door.

Defeated, I walked over to a small chair on the porch. I sat and waited. And waited.

Finally, as it was getting dark, I heard the sound of Mr. Woodcat's loose basket on the front of his bike rattle. I stood up and walked to the edge of the walkway as Mr. and Mrs. Woodcat peddled down the driveway with their baskets filled with groceries.

Mrs. Woodcat quickly put her bike down, ran over to me, and gave me a hug. She kept holding me as Mr. Woodcat put his bike on the bike rack and walked over to us.

"I'm so sorry, Ryko," Mrs. Woodcat said softly to me.

"Where are my parents? Are they OK?" I said, as I felt my eyes water.

Mrs. Woodcat released her hug and looked over at Mr. Woodcat.

He took a couple of steps closer and put his paw on my shoulder.

"Son, we don't know. No one knows for sure. We were gone for the entire summer on vacation. In fact, we left just a few days after you," Mr. Woodcat said, as he looked at the ground.

"I don't understand," I said. "What happened? Are my parents OK?"

Mrs. Woodcat bent down onto her knee and looked at me. "Ryko, we got back just a few days ago and saw that everything was burned. We haven't seen your parents. We've asked everyone in town. No one has."

I meowed loudly, began to cry, and Mrs. Woodcat caught me as I fell to the ground.

That was the darkest day and night of my life.

ENTRY 34

OVER THE COURSE of the next several weeks, I knocked on nearly every single door in town. I spoke to everyone that I could, asking if they knew or heard anything about my parents. I went everywhere. No one had any answers.

I made a few posters and hung them around town, hoping that someone, anyone would have some information for me. I never heard a thing.

Mr. and Mrs. Woodcat offered to let me stay in an extra room in their home for the winter, but I declined. I had been sleeping in the old woodshed by my house that was untouched by the fire. I just felt the need to be alone. I guess because I had never felt so alone.

One morning, I woke up shivering and looked out the small window. The first snowfall.

As I watched the snowflakes slowly fall from the sky, I laid there pondering deeply, really for the first time since I had walked into my yard and saw what was left of my home. My parents' home.

I reached over and pulled a blanket over me. I had no motivation to get out of bed. I had no motivation to do anything. I thought about my parents, and I also thought about myself. I started to ask the tough questions that I had been avoiding.

"What if they never return? What do I do with myself? What do I do with my life? Where do I go? Do I stay here and wait? For how long?" I asked myself

I didn't have any answers. I just let the questions play over and over again in my head like a broken record, as I continued to look out the window and watch the snow fall from the sky.

My eyes drifted downward to the table under the window. On the table were a few tools, a wooden box full of bolts and nails, as well as my backpack. I looked at my backpack and without giving it much thought, I got out of bed and took out my *Whisker Hollows* book. Then I crawled back into bed.

I took a deep breath, turned to the first page, and started reading.

ENTRY 35

THE SUN WAS SETTING and it was getting dark. There was just enough light to see as I turned to the last page in the book. I read the first four lines out loud:

"Scattered chaos; life unfulfilled,
Dreams broken, an urge to rebuild.
Darkest night; unbearable days,
Gives birth to light, casts self ablaze."

"Darkest night, unbearable days," I said as I thought about how life had been over the past few weeks.

I then read, "Gives birth to light, casts self ablaze," out loud. I started thinking about what York had said: "The journey is both down and up."

I read the poem down, then up. Down, then up over and over until I could no longer see the words as the darkness set in.

Each time I read the lines, I felt a new, more profound understanding and connection to the words than the time before. I jumped out of bed, grabbed my backpack, and left the shed.

As I walked, I could see my breath in the moonlight. I looked up to the clear sky filled with stars as the frigid breeze ran through my hair. "Rustling stars; prevailing breeze," I said to myself softly.

The loneliness I felt penetrated parts of my soul I did not know I had. It was deeper than lonely. I felt completely empty. I was hollow. I was... Nothing.

The strange thing about this degree of loneliness is that at first it really hurts. And I mean hurts more than any other type of pain imaginable. But slowly, too slow to even realize, that pain becomes a numbness that completely covers you like a blanket. You become physically and emotionally numb from head to toe. You feel nothing. Emotions just stop running through you. And not just negative emotions, every emotion goes away.

My fire was out. Kory had not crossed my mind. I hadn't thought about Whisker Hollows or my journey at all. I thought about literally nothing. I did nothing. I felt like nothing. This was without a doubt, my bottom of bottoms.

I continued to walk into the night. Suddenly, an idea popped into my head. It was more of a feeling than an idea, but whatever it was, it was the first thing I had felt in weeks. I knew that I needed to get out of there.

I turned around and started heading back towards home. Instead of going to my shed, I walked up to another driveway. I knocked on the door, and Mrs. Woodcat answered. "Ryko, it's so good to see you. Come in, come in. It is cold," she declared as she backed out of the doorway to allow me to walk in. "Let me make you something warm to eat and drink and please, have a seat at the table," she said walking toward the kitchen.

I took off my backpack, set it on the floor, and then sat at the table. I reached down and took out my journal. I grabbed my pen, opened my journal up, and started writing.

After a few minutes, Mrs. Woodcat came to the table with a large cup of warm milk and a heaping bowl of shepherd's pie. "Thank you, Ma'am," I said with already a spoonful of food in my mouth.

I continued to write as Mr. Woodcat walked into the kitchen. "Ryko, I haven't pushed it at all, but I feel I must. Please stay with us for the winter. It is getting far too cold for you to stay in a shed."

I kept my nose down to the paper in front of me and continued to write. "Mr. Woodcat, I can't tell you how much I appreciate your offer, but I have to decline," I said. Perhaps Mr. and Mrs. Woodcat could sense that I needed to pour my soul onto those pages because neither said another word to me and they walked back into their living room.

They left me alone for the next few hours as I continued to write in my journal. When I was finished, I carefully tore out all the pages that I had just written and folded them in half.

I wrote, "Mother and Father" on the front of it.

I slid my journal back into my backpack, put it on, and stood up from the table. "Mr. and Mrs. Woodcat?" I called out while picking up the folded pages.

"Yes, Ryko?" Mrs. Woodcat inquired as she walked into the kitchen, followed by Mr. Woodcat.

"I realize that this may not make any sense to you, but I must leave now and go to the train station. If my parents return, please give them this." I handed Mrs. Woodcat the large stack of paper. "It explains everything, as well as several ways for them to reach me, including names and addresses of people who know me."

Mr. Woodcat looked profoundly concerned. "Ryko, I don't know if it's a good idea to..."

Mrs. Woodcat cut him off. "Ryko, you do what you feel you need to do. You have our word that if or when your parents return, we will give them this letter," she said to me, followed by a warm smile.

I walked over to Mrs. Woodcat and gave her a hug. "Thank you," I said and I looked up at Mr. Woodcat. "And thank you, sir."

I then turned around, walked to the door, and stepped into the cold night.

ENTRY 36

THE TRAIN WAS NEARLY EMPTY, and I had a railcar all to myself. I had no particular destination; I just felt the urge to go somewhere. Anywhere. I got a traveler's ticket, which enabled me to ride the train and get on and off at any stops I chose for the next month.

I sat in a chair, put my head against the window, and fell asleep.

"Tickets, please!" a loud bellowing voice echoed in the railcar. I opened my eyes, through the window I could see trees passing by and mountains in the distance. It was bright outside. I had no idea what time it was or how long I had been asleep.

"Sir, I need to see your ticket, please," said the train worker. I handed him my ticket, and he quickly grabbed it with his paw. He looked at it, handed it back to me, and continued to make his way to the next railcar.

I stood up, stretched, and sat back down. And then I gave myself a bath, something that I hadn't done in I don't know how long.

I grabbed my backpack and removed my journal, my *Whisker Hollows* book, headband, tee-shirt, and the metal box I had taken from the burned cabinet, and I placed it all on the seat next to me.

I looked at my belongings, then back out the window. Then I noticed the seatbelt that was also on the seat. It was far too tangled for any cat to put on, and I wondered why they had seatbelts on the train. No one used them anyway.

Wait… Maybe I could actually use it.

I untangled the seatbelt, revealing the metal end that is supposed to snap into the other side of the lap belt, which I had yet to see. It didn't matter though because I had another idea.

Once there was enough slack, I situated the scorched metal box on my lap and gazed down at it. The word "Wildlife" was half missing, and the word "Binoculars" was completely gone. I picked up the seatbelt, put the metal edge on the side of the box, and pushed with all my might.

There were a couple of crackles and then a bang as the box popped open. The cover went flying into the air and landed on the seat with my possessions.

I focused my attention on the contents of the box, and my eyes watered. Inside, wrapped with a rubber band, were the postcards that I had mailed my mother and father.

I grabbed them with my paw and looked inside. The box was empty. I put the metal box on the seat in front of me. "My postcards," I said to myself tenderly. A few tears ran down my cheeks as I removed the rubber band. I thought about my mother and father reading the cards and imagined them laughing at my drawings and what I wrote.

I reminiscently looked at each one as memories of my journey flooded back. Denver, Colorado. Redondo Beach, California. Edmonds, Washington. Anchorage, Alaska. And Memphis, Tennessee. "Kory," I said. "I need to write to her."

I leaned forward and placed the postcards on the seat in front of me, but not far enough. They fell onto the floor. As I started to reach for them, I froze and my jaw dropped. "No way," I said to myself.

As I looked at them on the floor, I saw that they were slightly fanned out, revealing just the first couple inches on the left of each card. The letters spelled out: "D"... "R"... "E"... "A"... "M." Unable to divert my eyes, I remained paralyzed by bewilderment.

Then, slight tingling sensations washed over my entire body like a slow-motion wave. I could feel the hairs on my neck begin to stick straight up.

I picked up the postcards and spread them out in my paws. "This has to be a sign," I said to myself. "I need to write this down." Reaching for my journal, I realized that the metal lid landed on top of both my journal and *Whisker Hollows* book.

As I moved my paw to pick up the lid, what I saw stopped me in my tracks like a deer in headlights. The lid was covering the word *Hollows* on the book. All you could see was *Whisker*. And the only part of the Wildlife Binoculars logo that the fire had not destroyed was the word "life".

"Whisker Life," I said out loud. "Whisker Life. Dream." I felt another wave of tingles, but this time it was so intense every single hair stood straight up on my body. I was one giant puffball. I sat there perplexed for several minutes as the tingles and raised hair gradually subsided.

I hurriedly grabbed my journal and pen, opened up to a blank page, and wrote "DREAM" on the top. And then I wrote "WHISKER LIFE" below it.

I looked down at the page for a moment and then out the window. What happened next is something I had never experienced before, and to this day have only heard about happening to a few cats.

Some may call it inspiration, some may call it a big "ah-ha moment," and others may call it a "lightbulb moment." But to me, these descriptions fall very short. It couldn't have lasted more than a few seconds, but it felt like some sort of awakening, energy blast, or a direct download. I felt an incredibly bright light beam focused right on the top of my head. As the light hit me, it felt like thousands, no, millions of thoughts and ideas for Whisker Life hit me all at once.

And just as soon as it started, it stopped. My entire body felt energized, but thankfully I did not become a giant furball this time.

Not only did I feel energized, but the absolute bone and soul-crushing heaviness that I had been feeling was gone. Not minimized, it was completely gone. Literally, in just a few seconds, the way I had been feeling was just somehow gone in an instant. My mind was completely clear to a degree of clarity I had not previously experienced. The intense focus that accompanied the clarity was also unprecedented.

Without even thinking, I started to write down all the thoughts and ideas that I had as quickly as I could. Several hours passed by, before I reached the last page of my journal. But I had more, much more to write down.

I couldn't believe how amazing I felt. Yes, of course, I missed my mother and father more than words could describe. But somehow it was easy for me to completely separate my thoughts and emotions. I could visualize my parents as well as my feelings and emotions all inside a box in my head. It was as if I was able to detach myself from my emotions and choose how or what I wanted to feel. It was surreal.

As I sat down my thoughts kept coming in left and right about Whisker Life. I started to get a little nervous that I was going to forget some things before I had time to get more paper. I closed my eyes, released that nervousness, told myself that everything would be okay, and it was.

ENTRY 37

"Next stop, New York City," a voice blasted over the speakers. I wondered why they had the volume up so loud. My ears were ringing.

"Perfect!" I thought, "I'm going to hop off the train and buy some paper, maybe another journal. And some envelopes. Yes, envelopes! I have some letters to write and mail."

Once the train came to a stop, I walked onto the platform and climbed a long set of stairs. I reached the top of the stairs and found myself outside. Immediately, I was surrounded by cats passing this way, that way, and every which way. Everyone seemed to be in such a hurry.

I looked up and felt like a tiny ant as I was surrounded by giant buildings as far as the eye could see. "Wow," I said.

I started walking, or shall I say bouncing off one cat after another, as I tried to make my way to some shops I had caught a glimpse of through the crowd. I walked into a store and browsed stacks of different types of paper.

As I shopped, I was still trying to make sense of what had happened to me on the train. How is it possible that I could go from the lowest low I have ever felt to being at peace in the matter of a few seconds? And where are all of these ideas for Whisker Life coming from? I decided that I didn't care too much as to how it happened, I was just so grateful that it did.

I made my way over to a wall full of journals. There were well over one hundred to choose from. They ranged from cheap ones that looked like they were falling apart to journals that looked like they were fit for a king, and only a king could afford. I went for the thickest and cheapest one to save money and I also picked up some envelopes and loose paper.

Back on the street, I zigged and I zagged around all the cats rushing by me. This was a busy place. Thankfully there was a small park across the street with a few benches. I decided to go over to it, so I could continue writing about this new Whisker Life idea.

I found a somewhat clean bench and sat down. Remembering my ordeal in Denver, I decided to take out my pen and leave my backpack on. I opened my new journal and began to write. Words flowed from me like a waterfall. Wait, bad choice of words. I'm not reliving that experience. Words flowed from me like a calm, easy flowing stream, that had zero waterfalls nearby.

"Hiss Brands," an older cat said, as he sat on the bench right next to me.

I looked over to the cat, smiled, and said, "Pardon me?"

"The journal you are writing in - it's a Hiss Brands product," the cat said.

I closed the cover to look and there it was... the good old Hiss Brands logo. Honestly, it meant absolutely nothing to me because the Hiss Brands logo is on tons of products. From my backpack to toys I played with, some food products, and many other things. I've seen it since I was a kitten. In fact, there was a massive billboard right across the street from the park advertising Hiss Kitty Litter.

"Where are my manners?" the cat said. "Name's Mittens. Don't ask. Long story." He then pulled up his sleeve to show me his fur. All the hair on his body was black, except for his white paws. I didn't need to ask about his name; I quickly figured it out.

"Nice to meet you, I'm Ryko," I said as I looked back down at my journal so I could continue to write down my ideas.

"You see that tall black building over there?" Mittens said as he pointed down the street.

I looked up from my journal to see where Mittens was pointing. "You mean that one with the dark windows?" I asked.

"Yes, that's where I used to work until a year ago," Mittens said as he looked down to the ground. "I got fired you know. Not for doing anything wrong. No, no. Not at all. It was for trying to do something right."

"I'm sorry to hear that," I said. I took a deep breath and started to think of a way I could wrap up the conversation without being rude. I really needed to get back to writing.

"Korban Hiss. Rather Mr. Hiss, as everyone calls him. Most ruthless man in the world. Not a kind hair on his body, that's for sure. He was my boss," Mittens said as he rubbed his paws together.

"Look, Mittens, I'm really sorry, but I really need to…" I was cut off.

"Mr. Hiss is a dangerous man." Mittens turned towards me. "Look, kid, let me tell you something about that little journal you're writing in. I designed that. In fact, I created a lot of things you've seen and probably own. That building right there, that is Hiss Brands headquarters."

"Wait, you designed this journal?" I said as I closed the cover again to look at the Hiss Brands logo.

Mittens nodded his head and replied, "Journals, bags, book covers, many of the products you see out there today. I even designed that billboard in front of us. And even the HissBrands.com website. For twenty years I gave my life to Hiss Brands. For twenty years I played a game that I didn't even know I was playing. Once I found out what was really happening, I tried to warn a few co-workers, and I was fired immediately."

"Warn them about what?" I asked as I felt myself getting sucked into the conversation.

"Listen, all Mr. Hiss cares about is money, power, and control. That is it. And I mean truly, that is all he thinks about, wants, and he will do anything to gain more of it. Let me tell you a very big secret… one that will make you second-guess buying a Hiss Brands product ever again." Mittens reached into his pocket and took out a piece of paper and unfolded it.

"Look at this," Mittens said, as he handed me the paper. On it was a list of a couple dozen products that are under the Hiss Brands corporation. Under each name was an arrow pointing to the next one. "It's all connected," Mittens explained. "And I can't believe this was going on under my nose for twenty years. Let me explain."

Mittens took the paper back and inhaled an overly deep breath before he began, "Hiss Brands owns these newspapers. He puts bad news in the papers to sell more papers, which in turn, makes cats buy more Hiss Sour Milk, you know, to forget the bad news. They drink more sour milk, get an upset stomach, have to use their litter box more, so they buy more Hiss Kitty Litter. Then cats go to the store to buy medicine to feel better. You guessed it. Hiss Stomach Medicine. The medicine helps their stomach, but little do they know, there is something in the medicine that makes their claws grow faster, so they need to buy more scratch posts and claw cutters. And who owns the companies that make Meow Meow Scratch Posts and the Clawtastic Cat Claw Cutters? Any guesses Ryko?"

"Hiss," I said. And frankly, it wasn't a guess. I grew up sharpening my claws on the Hiss scratch posts Mittens was talking about. And of course I owned a pair of the Clawtastic Claw Cutters. What cat doesn't?

"Right!" Mittens said as he tapped on the paper with his paw. "And this is just one of the dozens of little systems that Mr. Hiss has set up to make more money and gain more power. This is only scratching the surface. You see, I know more, so much more. In fact, and I know this is going to sound crazy, but he plans to take over the world," Mittens said as his eyes got large, and he just glared at me.

I sat there, trying to absorb everything Mittens was telling me. "This is a crazy story, and may I ask why you're telling me all of this?"

"Because you are supporting Mr. Hiss by buying Hiss Brands products. You're supporting his mission, and I feel it is my mission to tell the real story behind the story to everyone I see with a Hiss Brands product. He must be stopped!" Mittens said as he pounded his paw on the bench.

I saw that as my cue to exit the conversation. I closed my notebook and put it back in the bag. "Mittens, it was a pleasure talking to you, but I must go and catch my train," I said as I stood up.

"Wait," Mittens said. "I don't expect you to believe me. I don't expect anyone to believe me. Do your own research. If you dig into Mr. Hiss' past, especially his great, great, great catfather who started Hiss Brands, you will see that it's all true." Mittens reached into another pocket. "Here, take this. I pass out hundreds of these booklets each day. It will help you research. You will see that everything I have told you is true."

Mittens handed me a paw-made stapled booklet with the title, "The Real Story Behind Hiss Brands."

I took the booklet and put it into my bag. "Thank you, Mittens. I truly wish you the best."

As I walked back to the train station, my mind danced between the crazy story I just heard and all the ideas for Whisker Life. I needed to get to a quiet place. And fast.

ENTRY 38

As I waited for the train to arrive, I pawed through the booklet that Mittens had given me. Inside, there were a dozen or so diagrams like the one he had shown me. The diagrams showed the companies and media outlets Hiss Brands owned, arrows pointing to their money-making schemes, and explanations next to each one. "That poor cat has gone mad," I said to myself.

I reached the last section of the booklet that had an image of the HissBrands.com website and a photo of Korban Hiss, who owns Hiss Brands today. Under that was his father, then grandfather, then great grandfather, and so on, through several generations.

The next page had a very old black and white photo of a small building with "Hiss Publishing" on the top, and a cat standing out front, holding a money bag. Under the photo, it said, "Mr. Hiss, Founder of Hiss Publishing."

I thought for a moment. "Hiss Publishing." How do I know that name? Out of *curiosity* (yes, I know the saying and was careful), I unzipped my backpack and pulled out the *Whisker Hollows* book carefully so no one around me could see. I flipped open to the first page, and my eyes nearly popped out of my head. In small letters, on the bottom of the page, it read, "Printed by Hiss Publishing, New York."

I quickly zipped my backpack and put it back on. "I don't understand," I said to myself. But I knew the one person in the world who would.

ENTRY 39

WHEN I BOARDED THE TRAIN IN NEW HAMPSHIRE, I literally had no plans or destination. I just felt the urge to leave New Hampshire right away and I never thought in a million years that I would be heading back to Whisker Hollows.

I had a few days, so I planned on using each and every minute wisely. I spent the entire first day continuing to write all of my plans and ideas for Whisker Life. What started as just a name soon developed into a roadmap for building a global company that would have a positive impact on the lives of millions of cats around the world. It would bring joy, laughs, and happiness. And it would play a very large role in helping cats get rescued and adopted.

I had no idea how to turn these thousands of ideas into reality, but at least I had everything written down. I smiled because I knew York would be proud when I told him I figured out "How" to accomplish my mission, my purpose, and my dream. Now exactly

"How" to get Whisker Life going was an entirely separate challenge I was hoping that was not the "How" York was referring to.

I decided to let that one sit, as I had a lot of letters to write. I wrote letters to Orky, Kyro, and Roky. Each letter was roughly five pages long. I wrote about my journey and what happened when I got home. Each time I wrote about everything that happened, I had to relive it.

Finally, I wrote a letter to Kory. Her smile. The way she ran her paw through her hair. All those emotions came bubbling back to the surface as I wrote to her. It wasn't my intention, but I shared a lot of details with her. After all, if it wasn't for Kory, I would not have abandoned my map and allowed my heart to guide me on my journey, which ultimately led me to Whisker Hollows.

For some reason, I felt I needed to keep the name Whisker Hollows out of the letters. Maybe it had something to do with learning how rare my *Whisker Hollows* book is from Roky. Or maybe it was because of the strange connection between the *Whisker Hollows* book and Hiss Brands.

Either way, it drove me crazy that I felt it wasn't safe for me to tell Kory all about Whisker Hollows in the letter. I wanted to share everything with her. But instead, I told her that I found a place that she had to see to believe. And, of course, I shared the exciting news about Whisker Life and a few significant ideas that I had for the new adventure.

I licked, sealed, and addressed all the envelopes. I put the envelopes inside my backpack to mail at the next stop. Then I opened the side pocket in my backpack, took out the purple rock from Whisker Hollows, and held it in my paw. I held it up to the light coming in from the window and watched the tiny colorful beams of light dance on the surface.

"What is that?" Said a booming voice to my right. I was so startled that I flew off my seat, sprang into the air, banged my head on the ceiling, and the purple rock slipped from my paw.

I landed back on my seat, followed by the purple rock, which landed on the seat between my legs and then rolled onto the floor.

"Oh, goodness," said the cat standing by my seat. "I didn't mean to scare the poop out of you." I looked up and saw a cat dressed in a suit, the same type of suit everyone was wearing in the streets of New York City. He was looking down at the rock on the floor.

I hastily bent over, picked up the rock, and hid it in my paws. "Um, that's not my poop. I mean it's not anyone's poop." I promptly put the purple rock back into my backpack. "It's actually not poop at all."

"Is that yours?" asked the cat, as he pointed his paw at the seat next to me. I looked and saw a paper bag with the word "lunch" written on it.

"No, that is not mine," I replied. Without hesitation, the cat reached down, picked up the bag, and scurried down the hallway into the next rail car.

As I turned to look out the window, I felt a slight tapping on the back of my seat. I turned to look, but no one was there. The tapping soon turned into a repeating *thump, thump, thump* that pushed into my back.

I looked around again; still, I saw no one. I then sat up a little and glanced back at the seat behind me. There sat a little white kitten, smiling and peering back at me with his giant black eyes. He started to kick the back of my seat again and started giggling.

I shook my head no and slowly moved back down into my seat. A few moments later, there was a much stronger *bang, bang, bang* that dug right into my back. Then a newborn kitten in the seat in front of me started crying as the bottle her mom was feeding her went dry. Further down the railcar, a cat began singing way offkey out of the blue. My head was about to explode.

I was very much looking forward to getting off that train, so I decided to get off at the next stop, no matter where it was.

ENTRY 40

WHEN THE TRAIN STOPPED, I darted off with a sense of urgency. My nerves were shot and I needed some peace and quiet. I ended up getting off the train a few stops before the one closest to Whisker Hollows. Heading out of town, I found a mailbox and dropped off the letters I had written to my friends.

When my paws hit the open trail, I felt peace wash over me. I actually welcomed spending a few days walking out in the forest. The weather was warmer since I was farther south and I needed some quality "me time".

As I walked, I spent a lot of time thinking about my mother and father. Not knowing anything was the hardest part. My mind bounced around from one scenario to the next. I didn't allow myself to dwell in these thoughts for long because I knew that path would lead to feeling so down that all I could do was lay in a cat bed.

Even though I had a lot of questions and concerns, I knew with every hair on my body that my parents would be so proud of me for how far I had come over the several months that passed. I learned a lot, as it had been one heck of a journey on every level imaginable and I felt that it was only the beginning of something amazing unfolding.

There were a few times that I had to stop to take out my new journal and write down ideas for Whisker Life that seemed to come to me out of nowhere. Don't judge me, but a few times, I put on the lime green headband that said, "PLAN TO WIN" from Kyro's event in Las Vegas. I don't know if it helped me or not, but I do know one thing; I was planning to win.

In order for me to win, I knew I had to do not just one, but dozens, even hundreds of things in order for me to have a positive impact on the lives of other cats around the world. I not only wanted to somehow help with rescues and adoptions, but kittens were also a big priority on my list. I needed to figure out a way that I could have a positive impact on their lives somehow, too.

In fact, one of the many ideas that I wrote down for Whisker Life was to write a book for kittens. That soon turned into two ideas for books, then five, then fourteen, and then the ideas just kept coming. Then the tagline for Whisker Life came to me, which is: "Love More. Hiss Less". And that's the way the whole process has been ever since the idea for Whisker Life came to me, well, shown to me.

Despite several things that were happening at that very moment in my life, I was happy and truly excited about what was in store for me.

ENTRY 41

As much as I'm sure you'd like me to, I cannot disclose the actual location of Whisker Hollows in this book. But what I can tell you is that there is a much easier way to get there than being swept away in a river, thrown down a waterfall, getting completely lost in the forest, and walking in circles for who knows how long.

Call it luck or instinct, but I knew the exact path to take to get to Whisker Hollows. Yes, it was the exact same path that I walked out, but still. I was pretty proud of myself for following a maze of trails and open forest to make it to that point.

Walking down a small trail, I knew I was getting close to Whisker Hollows because the air soon began to change to the sweet and crisp air I had grown to absolutely love.

Soon, I could see some trees glistening in the sunlight. And as I got closer, I could see the little hill and trail that lead up to the majestic oak tree and rock that had "Whisker Hollows" carved into it.

"York!" I yelled as I could see him sitting on the rock, looking out towards the valley. He didn't move a muscle and I realized he was probably catnapping. I slowed my walk as I approached York and noticed that the word "How" was not only still in the ground, but it looked very fresh. I looked over at York's walking stick and saw that it had fresh brown dirt on the bottom of it.

"Either York was expecting me, or he really needs to find a hobby," I thought jokingly.

"Sit, Ryko," York said gently.

I knew the drill and walked over to the side of the rock, put my backpack down, and sat on the ground.

"York, I have so much to tell you. When I got back..." I began to say, but York lifted his paw in the air towards me and I stopped mid-sentence.

"How?" York asked.

There were one hundred things I wanted to tell York and even more questions that I wanted to ask him, but I remembered the game. I feel bad for even calling it a game. It's not. It's just a way of communicating that requires one to thoroughly process what is said and to think before speaking. For someone who is a chatty-catty, it was not easy.

I proceeded to respond, but was having a hard time trying to condense how I came up with the Whisker Life concept, all the ideas for the adventure, and each of all the things that I wanted to do with it. I sat silent for a few moments. I decided to keep it simple and replied, "Whisker Life."

York turned towards me. "Tell me about this Whisker Life," he said.

He asked for it, so he got it. I told York the whole story. From the name to many of the ideas that I had for Whisker Life. I could tell he was getting excited. He would shift from the left and to the right and run his paws through his long beard and slightly close his eyes, absorbing each and every single word I said.

After several minutes, I just had to share what I wanted to

begin our whole conversation with. "York, please listen. When I returned to New Hampshire, everything was gone, including my parents. There are no signs of them anywhere. A fire destroyed our whole house."

York looked at the ground and took in a long, deep breath. He looked back at me with his deep, sparkling blue eyes. "I'm so, so sorry, Ryko. I understand and feel your deep pain." York leaned over and picked up his walking stick, placed it in front of him, and set both paws on it.

"When you are ready, we shall begin," York said as he slowly stood up.

"Begin what?" I asked.

"The next phase of your journey, of course," York responded with a wink as he walked by me. And then he stopped and turned back around towards me and added, "But give yourself some time, Ryko. Allow yourself to feel. Feel all of it. And then feel it again and again. Without feeling, there is no being. Without being, there is no meaning. Feel. And then be."

As York walked away, I allowed his words to dwell within me and I understood the deeper meanings behind what he said. I took a deep breath, stood up, grabbed my backpack, and started walking towards the valley of Whisker Hollows.

ENTRY 42

PEACE. That is the only word that comes to mind to explain what spending two days and nights just being and catnapping in the valley of Whisker Hollows feels like. I finally allowed myself to feel. I held nothing back. I shed many more tears. I asked the tough questions, and I allowed the tough thoughts to circulate through my mind over and over until they wore themselves out.

I felt centered, grounded, and at peace. Most of all though, I felt so grateful and happy for my journey and what was in store for me. I realized that many trees would fall across my path throughout my journey. Some trees are small enough to walk over. Others take a lot of work to clear. And a few completely cut off the path and a new route through the unknown must be found.

Learning to accept and be at peace removes so many of the worries. Instead of worrying about all the things that could happen, what if I focused on what I wanted to make happen?

As I walked over the rolling hills and made my way towards the majestic oak tree on top of the hill, I truly felt a profound shift within me. It's hard to put a finger on exactly what it was, but something was there.

I reached the top and didn't see York anywhere around so I walked down to his little house. I reached my paw to open the door just as it swung open. York was standing there with a big smile on his face. I looked at him, smiled back, and said, "I'm ready."

York turned around and made his way into the kitchen. I walked inside and closed the door behind me. "Sit, sit," York said while making a bunch of noise in the kitchen.

"So, York," I said. "If you are making tea, would you mind not making mine so hot?" I said. I was very thirsty and really wanted a drink to quench my thirst.

I walked over to the small table by the woodstove and sat down. Moments later York set down a cup of tea for me and another for himself. He walked around the table and sat down.

I reached for my cup and put my paws on the handle. "Ouch!" I said. The cup felt even hotter than the last time. I figured York didn't hear me about not making my tea so hot or perhaps he thought I said to make it even hotter. Ugh. So thirsty.

We sat silently for a moment. The awkwardness I felt during these moments of silence wasn't anywhere near what it was like the first time I met York. But still, they made me feel uneasy.

"Find another way," York said.

My mind began turning... Find another way with what? Whisker Life? That's not the way? I thought he liked it. Find another way... I had no idea.

"I'm sorry, find another way with what?" I asked.

York laughed a real York laugh. That was the first time I had heard what his laugh was like and it was great. In fact, hearing his laugh made me laugh. As I began to laugh, his face quickly turned serious. "If something is not working and you really want to accomplish a goal, you have to find another way," York said, as he looked at my cup and then back at me.

I looked at my cup for a few seconds. "Another way. What's another way with my cup?" I thought to myself. I then reached out my other paw and touched the side of the cup. It was cool to the touch. I picked up the cup, took a sip, and the tea was perfect. Not hot and not cold. I accepted this as a powerful lesson to always look for new ways around a problem.

For the next several hours, York and I discussed Whisker Life. I took out my journals and shared my plans and ideas. He shared some of his own ideas and tips, which I not only appreciated, but I took notes like crazy.

York also made me an offer to consider, an offer that I was completely floored by. He said if I made Whisker Hollows the headquarters of Whisker Life, he would share the secrets and knowledge that he has found there, with me. These secrets and knowledge would have a direct impact on Whisker Life and help ensure the missions would be accomplished. He told me not to answer and to take some time to think about it. I already knew my answer, but I told York that I would take some time to consider his offer.

I pulled out York's *Whisker Hollows* book and opened it to the first page. I also took out the small booklet that the cat gave me in New York City. I explained the story that I was told and showed York the photo of Mr. Hiss standing in front of the first Hiss Publishing building.

York took quite some time before responding. At first, I thought he was preparing his thoughts, but I realized that he was giving me time to prepare for what he was about to tell me.

ENTRY 43

YORK TOLD ME that many, many generations ago, Korben Hiss started a small book publishing company in New York City. At the same time, he had other interests in the import and export business. Back then, there were essentially zero rules, zero customs, and pretty much anything went. He made a lot of money back then.

The more money he made, the more power he had, and after a taste of this money and power, he couldn't get enough. This greed and power-hungry mentality was passed on to his son, who ended up taking over the business. His son continued to build and expand the business at all costs. He developed a reputation of being ruthless, cunning, and someone who you did not want to mess with in the business world or on the street.

Korben Hiss II created the holding company called "Hiss Brands" and started buying up all sorts of businesses, including as many newspapers as he could. He learned that whoever controls the media controls the minds of cats. And whoever controls the minds of cats can control their spending.

It was around this time that York sent the *Whisker Hollows* book to Hiss Publishing to see if they were interested in publishing it. They accepted it, printed several thousand copies, and sent them to bookstores around the country.

Before long, cats read the book and packed their bags to find Whisker Hollows. Many went alone, while others went in large groups. Those cats started to think more independently, started to dream of a new life, and did not buy as many newspapers as they did before, which Korben Hiss II did not like one bit.

Hiss wanted to put a stop to everything that was happening immediately, so he posted ads in all of his newspapers and put signs on lamp posts in city streets. The ads said that if you mailed the *Whisker Hollows* book back to the publisher, they would refund ten times the book price. The plan worked perfectly. Cats were running around everywhere, gathering all the books, and mailing them back in. The rumor was he bought all of the books back.

It was also rumored that Korben Hiss II then took all of the books and locked them up in one of their storage facilities in New York City. Another rumor is that he burned all of the books, except one.

Each generation of Hiss produced more and more ruthless and power-hungry cats. Leading all the way up to today. Hiss Brands now has their hands in nearly every industry and has hundreds of their evil profit systems in place. Driven by their control over the media, and all working together to serve one single purpose...

To take over the world.

What the cat told me in New York City was one hundred percent true and accurate. Hiss Brands is evil. They have a sinister plan to control everything and every cat all around the world to gain more money, more power, and more control.

My brain hurt. Before I left to let all of this information sink in, York leaned over to me, put his paw on my shoulder, and looked deep into my eyes. "Balance, Ryko. Keep Whisker Life under the radar. Hiss Brands cannot find out the true purpose. But at the same time, you need to grow quickly to spread happiness, laughs, and love. Balance."

"Yes, balance," I said as I walked out the door. My head was spinning so much from our conversation. Balance was something I had very little of as I stumbled down the walkway, tripped, and fell. Thankfully into a pile of leaves.

ENTRY 44

SPENDING SEVERAL HOURS looking out into the valley of Whisker Hollows allowed me to digest everything that York and I talked about. I started asking questions that I wouldn't have guessed in a million years I'd be asking myself. Those big, "What if..." questions like: What if Whisker Life, and ultimately my purpose, is far larger than I could have ever imagined? What if it's not only to spread happiness and to leave loving paw prints on the hearts of millions of cats around the world? What if it's not only to help adopt and rescue cats in need? What if it's to save the world from Hiss Brands?

I almost laughed at the thought. "Me, Ryko, save the world," I said chuckling. But then I allowed myself to play with the idea, just for fun. The more love and happiness I spread through Whisker Life, the less hold Hiss would have on cats, minds, actions, and wallets. The more that cats read my books and saw the Whisker Life pictures, the less time they'd spend looking at the newspapers published by Hiss Brands. And the more I spread positive messages, the more cats will awaken to their purpose and choose happiness and love over any other options.

"Stop being silly, Ryko," I said to myself. "There are hundreds of millions of other cats in the world. Surely there is a much more qualified cat out there to save the world. I'm just a little cat from New Hampshire."

Then the tiny voice in my head said, "But what if…"

I stood up and locked up at the glistening leaves by the majestic oak tree next to me. I proclaimed out loud, "Whatever all of this means, wherever this leads, I'm going to give it all I've got. That's all I can do." I then turned around and started walking down the trail heading to town.

ENTRY 45

As I walked in the forest, I quickly realized that putting all the pieces together and taking action to carry out hundreds of great plans is confusing and overwhelming. To be honest, I wasn't quite sure where to start.

"Do I start making Whisker Life t-shirts? Do I start writing books for kittens? Do I start making Whisker Life coffee cups? If so, where and how?" I asked myself. I was perplexed.

When I got to the town not far from Whisker Hollows, I decided to go to the post office where I had set up a mailbox earlier, to check if I had received any mail. When I opened my mailbox, I nearly did a backflip when I saw that I had a letter. I quickly scratched it open and started reading...

How Would You Like To Pee More And Clean Less?

Introducing the next revolution in peeing. Are you tired of changing your litter box every few days? How would you like to keep those beautiful claws of yours well-groomed and have more time to read the newspaper?

Our new Automatic Cleaning Litter Box 3000 by Hiss Litter Boxes Incorporated is now available to the public. The ACLB 3000 only has to be tended to once every 14 days, giving you the freedom to pee, worry-free!

Stop by your local Hissco store and pick yours up today. Bring in this letter and get 10% off - but only if you come by before Sunday.

Your friend,
Mr. Hiss
Hiss Brands
http://HissBrands.com

I don't know how I didn't see right through this before. I guess the same reason why every other cat doesn't see it. I crumpled up the advertisement and tossed it in the garbage. I closed my mailbox and was HEADING out the door when I heard, "Excuse me, are you Ryko?"

I turned around and saw a mailcat who was holding a small box in the air. "Yes, I am Ryko," I replied.

"Oh, good. I couldn't fit this package in your box. This is for you," the mailcat said as she walked over and handed me a package. "Oh good, thank you!" I told her.

I walked outside and sat on the bench that was in front of the post office. I carefully opened the package with my claws. Inside was a postcard and another small box.

I took out the postcard. On the front, it had "AUSTIN, TEXAS" in big letters. And under that it said, "Keep Austin Whiskery," whatever that meant. I flipped the card over and it said, "I believe in you, Ryko! - Kory"

My heart smiled. I opened up the small box and inside was an amazing red collar. Hanging off the collar was a tag that said, "WL" on it. I removed the collar from the box and there was a small note and long letter inside. The note said, "I hope you like it! The WL is for Whisker Life, as you probably guessed." The letter Kory wrote moved me to tears. She talked about my journey and how proud she was for me. She wrote about the fire, my parents, and how she wished she could comfort me during my difficult time.

I walked over to the window so I could see my reflection and put the collar on. I don't know if Kory made the collar too small, if I've gained a few pounds, or if the hair around my neck had grown. The collar was a bit tight. But I didn't care. I just looked at myself wearing the collar and smiled. "And so it begins," I said to myself.

In the reflection on the window, I noticed a store across the street that said "SOTOHP." I had never heard of such a thing and turned around to get a better look. "Ah, photos," I said. "Perfect."

"What adventure begins without photos?" I asserted to myself. "Certainly not Whisker Life!"

I walked across the street and went inside the photo store. "What can I do for you, good sir?" the store owner asked as he cleaned a large camera.

"I'd like to get some professional photos of myself, please," I answered while looking at all of the amazing photos of other cats on his wall.

"At your service. Name is Marty. Marty McCat," he said as he extended his paw.

"Nice to meet you. I'm Ryko," I replied.

"So we have all sorts of packages available. What do you need your photos for? For a special lady?" Marty asked with a wink. "To hang in your office? Thank you cards maybe?"

"I'm starting an adventure," I said with a big smile.

Marty had a big smile. "Ah, an adventure. I see. Well that's great to hear. I have just the package for you, it's our Adventure Promo Deluxe Package, which includes five photos, a logo for your adventure, plus a pack of ten stickers." Marty pulled out a book and opened to a page, showing an example of the package.

"I'll take it," I said.

"Purrrfect. Stand over here, and I'll start snapping the photos," said Marty, pointing to an area in front of the camera. Marty snapped a couple dozen photos and I picked out five that I liked. Then he asked me which one I wanted on my logo and I chose the picture of me sitting down.

"What's the name of this new adventure you're starting, Ryko?" Marty asked as he took out a piece of paper and a marker.

"Whisker Life," I said while taking my new journal out of my backpack. "I already wrote it out, but as you can see, it is far too small. Can you make it like this, but bigger?"

Marty looked at my cat scratch handwriting. "You got it, Ryko. Just give me about ten minutes, and I'll have everything ready for you to look at."

As I waited, I walked around the photo store and looked at some of the photos on the wall. I have to say, I was quite impressed by Marty's work. He obviously had a lot of skill.

"Marty, just curious, did you know that you wanted to be a photographer before your journey?" I asked.

Marty peeked over the desk where he was working. "Actually, no. I had no clue what my calling was when I left for my journey. But a funny thing happened, photography found me. I guess sometimes the path chooses you, rather than you choosing the path, if that makes any sense."

I laughed and replied, "That makes more sense than you know."

Marty stood up and walked over to the counter with a large envelope. "OK Ryko, let me know what you think of all of these. I'm happy to make any changes you need."

I opened the envelope and went over my five photos. They were perfect. Then I flipped over the last sheet, and my eyes got big. There was my Whisker Life logo with a picture of me sitting down. "It's perfect. In fact, they are all perfect. Thank you Marty," I said.

"You are more than welcome, Ryko."

I paid for my photos, walked out, and was ready for the next step in setting up my adventure. And that, of course, was… Well, unknown at that point.

ENTRY 46

BACK AT WHISKER HOLLOWS, my brain was more overloaded than ever before after another session with York. I was very impressed that York had quite a lot of knowledge about starting new adventures. He said it ran in his blood.

During our meeting, a lot of ground was covered. I brought up the fact that I had zero experience in this area. I had my photos, the Whisker Life logo, and a couple journals filled with ideas, but I was completely lost on what to do next. York offered to be my mentor and I immediately accepted.

I also shared my resounding "YES!" to York's previous proposal to make Whisker Hollows the official location where Whisker Life would be built. I felt ecstatic about my decision because there is no better place for it to be.

All of our planning got me thinking and questioning myself again. Before I left York's house, I asked him, "Why me? Couldn't another cat do something with Whisker Life?"

York replied, "Sometimes an idea chooses you, Ryko. There are trillions of ideas floating around, all around us. Most of the time we'll reach up, grab an idea, and think it's ours. Little do we know that many others can grab that same idea at the same time. And often, they do. But when an idea chooses you, Ryko, that is as rare as a diamond. When it happens, you know it in your heart and soul. It becomes your destiny to shine light upon the idea and give it life. For in time, that little idea will have a life of its own. You have been chosen, Ryko. This is your time to shine."

I swallowed hard, took a deep breath, and told York that I accepted my mission and that I would give it all I had.

Now, I must admit, I was quite nervous about York's advice on what I should do next. He suggested that I write a book, but not just any book. He suggested that I share my life story, leading all the way up to preparing Whisker Life for business. Putting yourself out there for the whole world to see is scary. Really scary. My mind tried to run wild with thoughts like:

"*What if no one likes my book?*
What if no one likes Whisker Life?
What if no one likes what we stand for?"

But I quickly shut down the fear-based questions floating around.

Instead, flipped them around to:

"What if everyone loves my book? What if everyone loves Whisker Life and what we stand for? In what ways will I positively impact the lives of other cats? And then the biggie... What if Whisker Life can really save the world from Korban Hiss and Hiss Brands?"

I decided to walk down to the Whisker Hollows valley. Once there, I sat under a tree next to the sparkling lake. It was so beautiful. Between the glistening light from the trees and sparkles from the lake, I felt like I was in one of those snow globes, but filled with glitter.

I needed to get my "WINNING" gameface on, so I reached into my backpack, pulled out my "PLAN TO WIN" headband, and put it on my head. Next I started to plan out my book, which, of course, is the very book that you are reading right now.

I settled on calling my book, *Ryko* because the other names I came up with wouldn't fit on the cover. One of my favorite choices was: *Ryko's Amazing Adventures: Discover How One Cat From New Hampshire Started A New Adventure That Would One Day Save The World From The Evil Mr. Hiss.* I still think it has a nice ring to it.

Then, thanks to York's help, I planned out how to promote my book. York suggested that I start sharing my story, along with some of my photos and sayings that I've come up with on Whiskerbook and Whiskergram.

Next, I moved on to creating designs for the products that I wanted to make and sell on the whiskernet at <u>whiskerlife.com</u>. My paws were crossed that cats would like my designs because Whisker Life sales would help me carry out my plans to save the world and help cats get rescued and adopted.

Finally, I moved on to writing out more details for all the kitten books that I plan to write. You would never believe the number of kitten books that I have mapped out. Let's just say that I'll be writing books in Whisker Hollows for many, many years to come.

So that's how Whisker Life got started, and now you know everything about me.

At the time of this writing, all I have is the Whisker Life name, a logo, and a dream. A dream that I hope I never awake from because I am finally ready to take action on my purpose, my mission, and my adventure. I'm ready to go after my dreams. I'm ready to make a real difference. I hope that my story inspires you to do the same. No matter how tough things get, always remember, you are here on purpose for a big purpose. Find yours. Own it. And go after it.

Thank you for taking the time to read my book. I wish I could hug each and every one of you and thank you in person. Truly, I mean it from the bottom of my heart, thank you.

Love,

Ryko

P.S... As you can tell, I'm a very curious, motivated, and outgoing cat that loves to meet other cats. I spend a lot of time thinking about how the world around me works and love to connect the dots to find deeper meanings in all things. You have likely also figured out that I'm also an emotional cat. So if you do decide to leave a review for this book (please do, they help!) on Catazon or another site on the whiskernet, please be gentle. I will read each and every review, and knowing myself, I will probably take everything to heart!

ABOUT WHISKER LIFE

What we do: We inspire people to fully live their life's purpose. To Love More and Hiss Less.

How we do it: By sharing stories, ideas, and inspiration to help you find and navigate down your path.

Who we do it for: Those who seek more love, passion, purpose, and positivity in their lives.

Why we exist: To spread love, happiness, and smiles. To leave tiny paw prints on the hearts of many. To help cats get rescued and adopted. And to be an inspiration to follow your dreams. Oh, and to save the world from an evil corporation.

HOW YOU CAN HELP

I would be crazy to think I could do this all by myself. In order to achieve the Whisker Life mission, I'm going to need a lot of help. If you believe in our mission, I kindly ask you to share Whisker Life with others Please like us and follow us on social media, and we will do our best to bring you lots of smiles, laughter, inspiration, and happiness.

Together we can make a real difference (and maybe even save the world).

Where to find us:

Whiskernet Website: http://whiskerlife.com

Whiskerbook: http://facebook.com/whiskerlife

Whiskergram: https://www.instagram.com/whiskerlife/

WhiskerTube: Search for: Whisker Life

.

Made in the USA
Middletown, DE
23 September 2021